"I know why you're really here."

Drake's gray eyes studied her face. "Why?"

Her voice growing husky, Allie said, "You were just looking for some excuse to chase after me!"

To her surprise, he nodded. "Yes, I'll admit to that. But you're not the kind of woman I thought you were."

She gave a throaty chuckle. "You were looking for a flesh-and-blood woman, who turned you on, so don't try and make out you were looking for something more. All you wanted was sex. You saw me, wanted me and set out to seduce me!"

SALLY WENTWORTH was born and raised in Hertfordshire, England, where she still lives, and started writing after attending an evening class course. She is married and has one son. There is always a novel on the bedside table, but she also does craftwork, plays bridge and is the president of a National Trust group. Sally goes to the ballet and theater regularly and to open-air concerts in the summer. Sometimes she doesn't know how she finds the time to write!

Books by Sally Wentworth

HARLEQUIN PRESENTS®

1856—CHRISTMAS NIGHTS
1882—MARRIAGE BY ARRANGEMENT
1902—THE GUILTY WIFE
1992—RUNAWAY FIANCÉE

SALLY WENTWORTH

Mission to Seduce

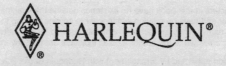

TORONTO • NEW YORK • LONDON
AMSTERDAM • PARIS • SYDNEY • HAMBURG
STOCKHOLM • ATHENS • TOKYO • MILAN • MADRID
PRAGUE • WARSAW • BUDAPEST • AUCKLAND

ISBN 0-373-12018-4

MISSION TO SEDUCE

First North American Publication 1999.

CHAPTER ONE

DAMN! Allie thought angrily, and exclaimed, 'But I won't need an interpreter.'

'Do you speak Russian?'

'Yes, as a matter of fact I do,' she said triumphantly. But then, as she looked into her boss's sceptical eyes, reluctantly added, 'A little.'

'How little?'

She gave him one of her sudden smiles, her blue eyes lighting with mischief. 'Enough to say no if I'm propositioned.'

He laughed, wanting to be serious but unable to resist her smile. 'But do you speak enough Russian to recognise a proposition if you hear one?'

'One could be deaf and dumb and still recognise *that*!'

He shook his head at her and said, 'I know you're a capable career woman and all the rest of it, but I'm not going to risk letting you loose in Russia without someone to keep an eye on you.'

Allie hated the sound of that; she had reasons—important and secret reasons—of her own for going to Russia that had nothing to do with the assignment she'd been given, and to have someone looking over her shoulder would be inconvenient to say the least. But it was important not to jeopardise the trip so, to keep the boss sweet, she smiled and said, 'OK, leave it with me. I'll find someone out there.'

'No need,' he said on a pleased note. 'I already know of someone based in Moscow. A family friend, I suppose you could call him. His name is Drake Marsden and he works for a bank that's opening up a branch over there. He speaks the language and will give you all the help you need. I'll have him meet you when you arrive.'

'Wonderful,' Allie enthused, while inwardly cursing, and she determined to get rid of this extremely unwanted man at the very first opportunity.

She thought that opportunity would present itself at Moscow airport. Surely in the bustle of a huge international concourse it would be possible to lose herself in the crowd, slip into a taxi and so free herself of her boss's pal right at the start. There was bustle, all right. Take the crowd outside Harrods on the first day of the January sale, double the amount of shoving and pushing, and even then it would only give a small idea of what it was like at Moscow airport. There was complete chaos, and that was before Allie even got through to the concourse. Everybody seemed to be flying in to Moscow that August day, and they were all herded into a great crowd that gradually developed into long queues of passengers waiting to have their visas and passports checked, the officials achingly slow and letting only one person through at a time.

Allie stood in the queue for over two hours, weighed down by her expensive camera equipment that she didn't dare rest on the ground in case it got

kicked by the people pressing all around her. A large
man stood on her foot, and a fat woman with elbows
made of steel tried to push in front of her, thinking
Allie a soft touch because she was so petite, but received a blazing look from angry blue eyes that
stopped her in her tracks.

The only compensation in all this, Allie decided,
was that Drake Marsden would certainly have given
up on her and gone home long before she got through.
Once past this barrier she had to join another queue
to change some money into roubles, retrieve her suitcase, and wait in yet another line to go through the
baggage check, so that it was over three hours before
Allie eventually emerged, tired, hot, and thirsty, into
the main concourse.

She didn't even bother to look for some middle-
aged man with a very fed-up expression holding up a
board with her name on it, but just headed for the
welcome open air and a taxi. There were a lot of taxis,
all looking equally old and unreliable, but, before
Allie could get a hand free to hail one, a modern sil-
ver-grey Mercedes, large and sleek, pulled up at the
kerb beside her. A man got out, quite young, tall and
lean, and with thick dark hair. Allie gave him a
glance, made a mental note that Russian men were
much better-looking than she'd expected, then dis-
missed him as she tried to attract the attention of a
taxi-driver by standing on tiptoe to look over the roof
of the Merc and wave.

'Miss Hayden?'

Allie blinked, and slowly turned. The man from the
Mercedes, in his immaculate dark suit, was looking

at her expectantly. She thought of denying her identity but there was no way this man could be a buddy of her boss, who was not only well into his fifties but had the middle-aged spread to go with it. 'Yes,' she acknowledged guardedly.

He held out a hand. 'I'm Drake Marsden. Welcome to Russia.'

Slowly, with inner chagrin, she put her hand in his and had it briskly shaken.

He was very businesslike, opening the passenger door for her, putting her case and camera equipment in the boot, ignoring the blare of an impatient taxi horn, getting in and driving away, all within a minute.

'How did you know it was me?' she asked, looking at the lean planes of his profile with very mixed feelings.

'I was given a description—and then there was all the photography stuff.'

Fleetingly Allie wondered how her boss had described her. Short, blonde, and sexy, probably, knowing him. She had been given no description of the man beside her, and as she had no intention of using him hadn't asked for one. But maybe it would have been helpful to know in advance that Drake Marsden was both good-looking and—judging by his clothes, the gold Rolex on his wrist, and the car—fairly affluent. His voice, too, was attractive, being deep and with the unmistakable accent of a good public school.

'I thought you'd have given up on me after the hold-up at the airport,' she remarked.

'What hold-up?'

She gave a small gasp. 'I was queuing in there for

over three hours! I thought the officials had gone on a work to rule, or something.'

Drake gave her an amused glance. 'No, it's always like that. I didn't bother to set out until long after your flight was due. Weren't you warned?'

'No, I wasn't,' she said feelingly.

To her annoyance, he laughed. 'That sounds like Bob,' he commented, naming her boss.

'Is he a close friend of yours?' she asked curiously.

'No, but he knows my parents quite well. They have a shared interest in horse-racing.'

So that explained the age difference, Allie realised, guessing that Drake must be in his early thirties, a whole generation younger than her boss. He hadn't asked her where she wanted to be taken to, so she said, 'I take it we're going somewhere in particular?'

'To your hotel.'

'I haven't chosen one yet,' she pointed out.

'I know, so I've booked you into the Baltschug Kempinski. It's an old building that has been restored and modernised, and it's handy for Red Square and the Kremlin.'

'I'd intended to stay at the Ukraine,' Allie said frostily, annoyed at his high-handedness.

To her further annoyance he gave her an amused, almost pitying look. 'Believe me, you wouldn't like it there. It's where all the Communist officials from out of town used to stay. And it's still very basic.'

'Perhaps I'd prefer to find that out for myself,' she told him stiffly.

Another amused glance came her way. 'Ah, you're

into this feminism thing, are you?' Drake remarked with casual chauvinism.

It was the kind of remark that immediately put her back up. Allie thought of telling him exactly what she thought of his attitude, but then shrugged inwardly and let it go; as she intended to ditch him just as soon as possible there seemed no point in setting him straight. But it made her decide at once that he was the sort of man she had absolutely no time for. One who was still trapped in the time-warp of gender stereotyping. Lord, he probably even thought that the little woman's place was still tied to the kitchen sink!

Giving him a sideways, and very prejudiced, glance from under her lashes, Allie had the momentary thought that it was a pity he wasn't her type, because she had to admit that his clear-cut features under level eyebrows were more than attractive. And he had the kind of tall, broad-shouldered but slim figure that made clothes look good on him, even elegant. When that adjective came into her mind it caught her by surprise; it wasn't one she often ascribed to a man but it fitted him exactly.

But if there was one kind of man she couldn't stand it was one who was narrow-minded in his attitude towards women. Allie had come across it too many times in the past. At first she had fought it, but had come to realise that most of the time she was beating her head against a solid concrete wall. The poor creatures had chauvinism ingrained into them from the cradle and nothing she could say or do would change it. So now she employed a more subtle method, and where necessary used the chauvinism for her own ends. And, looking at Drake Marsden, she decided to do the same now. To use him until she was ready to ditch him and go off on her own secret quest.

Smiling inwardly, she turned to look out of the window at this new country she'd read so much about. The roads were full of cars, mostly old Russian-built Ladas that belted out choking exhaust fumes, making Allie grateful they didn't have to have the windows open. The car had air-conditioning so was pleasantly cool, but outside the sun beat down on the streets full of sweltering people. It made her feel hot just to look at them. 'I thought it would be quite cool here,' she commented, slipping off her jacket, 'but it's hotter than England.'

'We seem to be having a heatwave at the moment, which is quite exceptional. In Russia they have a saying, "We spend nine months looking forward to the summer and then have three months of disappointment." So you're in luck.'

Drake steered the car expertly, completely at home in the congested traffic, she noticed. 'How long have you been out here?' she asked, for something to say.

'About six months.'

'And Bob said you speak Russian.'

'Yes, I took it as one of my subjects at university.'

An egg-head, she thought. Just her luck. 'I never went to university,' she said provocatively.

'Then you must be extremely good at your job to be given such a responsible assignment,' Drake commented.

Flattery and condescension all in one sentence! Lord, it would almost be a pleasure to take him down a peg or two, Allie thought tartly, and if all she'd had to think about was her assignment she might have taken the time to do it, just for the hell of it. But right now she had other, far more important things on her mind.

The streets widened into broad thoroughfares, the buildings became grander, and Allie gave a gasp of pleasure as she caught a glimpse of the first onion-domed church to come into view, the golden domes bright and beautiful against the clear blue of the sky.

'Wait till you see St Basil's,' Drake told her.

'St Basil's?'

'It's the cathedral in Red Square.'

They crossed the bridge over the River Moskva and Allie gave a delighted laugh as she saw the huge church with its brick-coloured towers, surmounted by a hotchpotch of domes. 'It's like something out of a fairy-tale!' she exclaimed. 'I had no idea there would be domes in so many different colours and patterns. The people who built them must have had a great love of colour.'

'They still have. They're a hot-blooded race.'

Allie thought she noticed a note of disapproval in Drake's voice, which amused her. If he disapproved of people with passion in their veins, then what did that make him? But perhaps he liked playing the austere Englishman.

It took them only another couple of minutes to reach the hotel. Drake parked outside and in a very short time had helped her check in and carry her stuff up to a very comfortable room, with a window from which she could see the patterned domes of St Basil's.

He glanced at his watch. 'You'll want to unpack, and I have some business that will take me about half an hour and then I'll meet you downstairs. Is there anything you need?' he asked her.

'I'd murder for a drink.'

He smiled at the feeling in her voice. 'Then I'll meet you in the bar.'

Not, 'Would you care to meet me in the bar in half an hour?', Allie noticed, just the arrogant assumption that he was in charge and she would have to fall in with his timetable. In a small act of defiance she opened the fridge that nestled under the built-in dressing-table and poured herself a soda, tilting back her head to savour its liquid coldness in her dry throat, the material of her blouse stretched across her breasts. After the first drink she gave a long sigh and licked her now cool tongue slowly over her parched lips. Glancing at Drake, Allie saw that his eyes were studying her, and she gave a small smile. 'I thought you had some business to do,' she reminded him.

He blinked, nodded, said, 'See you later.' And went swiftly from the room.

Although the building was old, the ceiling in the room high and corniced with ornate plasterwork, there was, thankfully, a very modern bathroom. Allie stripped off and stood under the shower to cool down, then padded around the room in her underwear while she unpacked her suitcase. There was a safe in the wardrobe and into it she put her valuables, and also a small but very important old notebook. Standing in front of the full-length mirror, she took her time in redoing her face and brushing the short blonde curls that clustered round her head like an angel's halo. She found a sleeveless sun top and a short denim skirt, put them on and looked critically at her reflection for a couple of minutes, wondering whether to make Drake fall for her. He was certainly interested, she knew that already. And it might be amusing.

But no, she decided, picking up her bag; if it got out of hand, if he got serious, it might make it difficult to get rid of him when the time came. Looking at her watch, she saw that she had already kept him waiting for nearly twenty minutes, so strolled down to the bar.

Drake didn't look at all put out by the wait, in fact was leaning against the bar chatting to another man in fluent Russian. He straightened when she came in, his eyes going over her and lingering just a little too long on her shapely legs. 'Hello. What would you like to drink?'

'Well, as I'm in Russia, I suppose it had better be vodka.'

'With tonic?'

'Please.'

Drake gave the order to the barman and saw that his companion was looking at Allie with unconcealed interest. 'Let me introduce you,' he said dryly. 'Sergei Morozov. Miss Alexandra Hayden.'

'Allie,' she said with a friendly smile as she extended her hand.

It was taken and enveloped in the large hand of a man almost as tall as Drake, but with heavier features that were good-looking in a florid way. He had fair hair, was wearing a brown suit, but had a look in his eyes that spoke of a more extrovert nature under the conventional exterior. He gave her a polite bow and she had to take her hand from his as he showed no sign of releasing it. 'Welcome to my country,' he said expansively, as if he owned the place.

'Why, thank you.' Both men towered over her five feet three inches, so to make things more equal Allie climbed up onto a bar-stool. There was a momentary silence as both men savoured her legs while she did so, then Sergei said in good English, 'You are on holiday in Moscow?'

Allie gave Drake a flicking glance, then, seeing no reason to prevaricate, replied, 'No, actually I'm here on business. I work for a computer information company, and we've been asked to put together material for a CD-ROM—a compact disk—on Fabergé.'

'On Fabergé?' He opened his hands in an extravagant gesture. 'Then you have come to the best place in the world. But there is so much information. The factory made so many beautiful things.'

'So I understand. But I'm concentrating on just the Easter eggs they made at the moment.'

'Ah, of course. Everyone wants to see the famous eggs.'

'I understand you have several here in Moscow?'

'Yes, certainly. At the Armoury museum.'

'That's in the Kremlin, isn't it?'

'You are well-informed, Allie.'

She smiled, but inwardly wondered if he really thought she would have undertaken a project like this without having first done her homework.

Drake said casually, 'As a matter of fact Sergei

might be able to help you. He has free access to the Kremlin.'

'You do?' Allie's eyes widened and she looked suitably impressed as she gazed at the Russian.

He preened himself a little. 'It is simply because of my work, you understand.'

'Oh? What do you do?'

'I am an architect, and an official in the department that deals with government buildings.'

'And quite a high official,' Drake put in.

Sergei smiled and didn't deny it, but went on, 'And as the Kremlin is the most important government building in Moscow I have to keep a close eye on it.'

'What a wonderful job,' Allie said with open awe, but wondering if she was overdoing it a little.

It seemed not. Sergei took her admiration as his due and said expansively, 'It will be my pleasure to show you over the museum.'

'How very kind of you. Actually I do have an appointment to meet a Professor Martos. I understand he's the curator in charge of the Fabergé eggs.'

'Ah, yes. I know him. I will speak to him and make sure he gives you all the help you need.'

'That's really very kind of you. I'm most grateful. I just know I'm going to have a wonderful time here.'

She smiled sweetly at the Russian and he became expansive, telling her about the delights of Moscow that she mustn't fail to see. After another half an hour and a couple more drinks that he allowed Drake to buy, he remembered he was supposed to be somewhere else and took himself off, first bowing low over Allie's hand. For a moment she thought he was going to kiss it but he contented himself with pressing it meaningfully while looking into her eyes in open admiration.

When he'd gone, Drake gave him five minutes, then said, 'Drink up. Let's get out of here.'

They walked out into the late afternoon sunlight and made their way to Red Square. For a while Drake pointed out the familiar landmarks that she'd heard of so often: the Kremlin with its high surrounding wall, the Gum department store opposite, and the angular red stone of Lenin's tomb.

There were quite a few people about, mostly groups of tourists, but it wasn't at all crowded. As they strolled along, Drake looked at her and said dryly, 'You handled Sergei very well.'

'He seems nice,' she said guardedly, and saw his mouth quirk in wry amusement. 'And wasn't that what you intended—that I should be nice to him?'

His head came round sharply and his eyes became intent. 'Not at all. I merely thought he might be useful to you.'

'Is he a friend of yours?'

'An acquaintance. Russians like getting to know foreigners. Both male—and female.'

There had been a definite pause and an inflexion on the last word that made Allie raise her head to look at him. 'Was that a warning?'

He nodded. 'Russian men tend to think it something to boast about if they can—get to know a European woman.'

'What do you mean by ''get to know''?' Allie lifted a guilelessly innocent face to his.

Quizzical grey eyes met her blue ones for a moment, then he said drily. 'I'm quite sure you understand me.'

To tease him she kept up the naive act for a little longer. 'Become friendly, do you mean? Let them show you round the city, that kind of thing?' For a second he looked uncertain, but then saw the amusement in her face. His expression stiffened a little and she laughed. 'You mean have sex, don't you?'

Drake nodded. 'To allow that to happen would be a very big mistake.'

She felt a sudden flash of anger at his presumption in warning her off. What kind of woman did he think she was, for heaven's sake? Did he think that she could be swept off her feet so easily? Did he think her so cheap that she'd allow herself to be seduced by some stranger, albeit a rather good-looking one? Or was it just that he had a low opinion of women in general and expected them to fall for every glamorous foreigner they met?

'Thanks for the warning,' she said shortly, adding on a falsely artless note, 'I'd never have known men could be so despicable if you hadn't pointed it out.'

His eyes growing contemplative, Drake said, 'May I ask you a personal question?'

'You can ask—but I don't guarantee to answer it.'

'How old are you?'

Her mouth creased in amusement. 'How old do you think?'

'In your mid-twenties?'

She nodded. 'Near enough. Why do you want to know?'

But he didn't answer, instead saying, 'And do you have a partner—isn't that how people in a lasting relationship are euphemistically described nowadays?'

'You sound as if you don't approve.'

'Of the wording or the relationship?'

She shrugged. 'Both.'

Drake looked at her for a moment, his face brooding and his eyes hidden under lowered lids, then he said, 'You haven't answered my question.'

Seeing that she'd only just met him that was hardly surprising, Allie thought indignantly. She said, 'I told you I didn't guarantee an answer.'

'And you're not going to?'

Tilting her head to one side as she looked at him, Allie said, 'I think—not.'

For a moment he looked annoyed, as if he wasn't used to being thwarted, but then his tone became brisk and formal again. 'Very well, as you wish. I'll walk you round to the entrance to the Armoury museum so that you'll know where to go when you visit.'

He led her round the side of the wall and through a gate in a low iron railing that led through an archway guarded by armed soldiers. Through it they came into an open area where a section of pavement in front of the main building had been given a cover supported by scaffolding poles. A means of keeping the rain and snow off the queues of tourists waiting to enter, Allie presumed. Today, though, it served the purpose of providing welcome shade from the heat.

'Isn't it open yet?' she asked, puzzled.

'Yes, but visitors are only allowed in at certain times and for a set period.'

'I hope that won't apply to me,' she said in some alarm. 'I'll need prolonged visits, preferably when there aren't any visitors around.'

'I dare say that can be arranged.'

Allie swept her eyes over him assessingly, wondering if he had any influence here. 'I understand your company is setting up a branch in Moscow,' she remarked casually.

'Yes, that's right.'

It was far from being a helpful answer, so she had to come right out and ask, 'What sort of business is it?'

'Banking,' Drake replied shortly.

So he was nothing but a glorified bank clerk. Dull stuff, and he certainly couldn't have any influence that would be helpful. He had probably already done the most that he could in introducing her to Sergei.

Turning, they left the Kremlin to walk back to her hotel. Allie had travelled a lot in the past, on holidays and with her job, so she was used to new countries. But Russia was somehow different. Perhaps the first thing she noticed was the road and street signs; they were completely impossible to decipher because Russia used the Cyrillic alphabet where some of the letters looked the same as the ordinary alphabet but had different meanings. An H for an N, for example. And then there was the beauty and colour of the splendid churches and the Kremlin, compared with the ring of concrete apartment blocks that surrounded the city.

'Is it safe to walk around alone here?' she asked idly.

She got a reaction she certainly hadn't expected. Drake stopped and spun round. 'What do you mean?' he demanded sharply.

Blinking in surprise, Allie said, 'Well…just what I asked; is it OK for me to walk around alone?'

Slowly his taut face relaxed and Drake ran a hand through his hair, but his voice sounded strained as he said, 'In the daytime, yes, but I would certainly advise against it at night. In fact, I insist that you don't.'

She gave a small gasp at his vehemence. Was the place that dangerous, then? Allie frowned, puzzled, but said nothing more. When they got to her hotel, she turned to Drake and held out her hand. 'Well, thank you very much for meeting me and everything. It was very good of you to take the time.'

'Not at all.' He shook her hand but didn't go, instead saying, 'You said you'd been in contact with Professor Martos. When do you intend to see him?'

'Some time tomorrow. I'm going to call him now to arrange a time.'

'Does he speak English?'

'Yes, I believe so.'

'Are you sure? Would you like me to help you make the call?'

God give me patience, Allie thought, but said with some irony, 'I think I might just be able to manage to make a phone call by myself.'

The sarcasm wasn't lost on him. Drake raised an eyebrow, but only said, 'Very well. I'll pick you up at eight to take you out to dinner.'

'That's very kind of you, but I really don't want to put you to any trouble,' Allie said hastily.

'It's no trouble.'

'But what about...?' She had been going to say 'your family', but intuitively knew that he didn't have anyone here, so changed it to, 'I'm sure you're terribly busy; I don't want to take up all your time.'

Drake frowned for a moment, then said curtly, 'I'll meet you in the lobby at eight.'

He walked to where he'd parked his car and Allie watched him drive away with great misgivings. Trust her to get landed with a chauvinist, and an autocratic one at that. When he'd gone, she made her call to Professor Martos from the phone in the lobby, then quickly strode back to the Gum department store.

The building reminded her strongly of a huge French château with its white façade and sloping green roofs, but inside it was a delight of galleried arcades linked by bridges, ornate iron railings, and stuccoed archways. Allie searched the shopping arcades for a store that sold maps in English and bought a road atlas covering western Russia, from Moscow north to St Petersburg. Only then did she take time to stop and admire the magnificent glass roof that spanned the store like some immense spider's web, the sun casting shadows that elongated the strands of the web and seemed to reach out to trap the shoppers as they passed below.

The shops were starting to close but Allie browsed through them, looking for typical Russian goods, but the up-market western companies seemed to have hijacked the place and if it hadn't been for the wonderful architecture she could have been in any shopping mall in any part of the world.

When she got back to her hotel Allie locked the road atlas inside her suitcase. It was unlikely that Drake would ever come up to her room again, but she didn't want to run any chance of him seeing the book and starting to ask questions. She changed into a beige lace dress that left her shoulders bare and, rather than have Drake call up to her room, went down to the lobby to meet him.

She reached it just as Drake was coming into the hotel. Allie caused quite a stir as she came out of the lift; most of the people glanced round and let their eyes linger. But then, it was a designer dress, and she knew she looked good in it, the colour and the style perfect for her slim figure.

Drake stood still for a moment and then walked forward to meet her. 'You're exactly on time,' he remarked, letting his gaze run over her.

'I don't usually keep people waiting for three hours,' Allie told him, referring to the wait at the airport.

He smiled, his grey eyes creasing with amusement. 'You're never going to forget that, are you?'

'Could anyone?'

'Don't let it put you off the country.' He put a hand under her elbow to lead her to the door.

'Oh, I won't.' She raised her hand to her hair, making him let go of her arm, and then strode ahead of him out into the open.

His car was waiting at the kerb and Drake opened the door for her. She wasn't sure whether or not he had got the message, but he made no further attempt to touch her.

'Where are we going?' Allie asked as he began to drive away from the city centre.

'To a restaurant where they do typical Russian food. I thought you might prefer that on your first night here.'

'How thoughtful of you.'

He gave her a somewhat sardonic look, one level eyebrow rising. 'Most people seem to.'

Which put her in her place, Allie thought, smiling inwardly. 'Do you live in a hotel?'

'No, I have an apartment, for the moment.'

'You intend to move?'

'No, but my job here is over. I shall be going back to England shortly.'

'Shortly?' Allie fastened on the word, wondering if it represented an easier way to get rid of him. 'I hope you're not staying on here in Moscow just because of me.'

Drake didn't answer directly, merely saying, 'I'm due some leave.'

Turning to look at him, Allie said, 'Good heavens, how embarrassing. I wouldn't for the world want to keep you from going home, from being with your family. In the circumstances it was wrong of Bob to ask you to—'

'I'm happy to do it,' Drake interrupted rather brusquely.

He said it in a tone that was meant to stop all argument, all further protestations, but Allie tried once more, saying with a little sigh, 'Bob really is a dear. He worries about me, and I appreciate it. But he never seems to get it into his head that I'm quite capable of looking after myself, even in a foreign country. I can just imagine the list of instructions he gave you.' She deepened her voice into a playful imitation of her boss's bass tone. 'Don't let her get too friendly with the natives. Make sure she knuckles down to work. Don't let her go off sightseeing—this isn't a damn holiday. And don't let her go on the Metro in case she gets lost. And don't let her loose in the shops or she'll spend a fortune.'

Pulling up outside the restaurant, Drake turned to her and laughed. 'How did you know what he said?'

'Because I got the very same lecture before I left, of course. Whenever he sends me on an assignment he always worries himself silly in case something happens to me.'

'I'm surprised he lets you go, then.'

Her voice becoming serious, Allie said pointedly, 'He has to. I'm good at my job and he knows it. And when it comes down to it, it's my expertise he wants and is paying for. Oh, he might put on the act of being paternal and worrying about my welfare, but maybe that's to compensate for the fact that he can't do the job himself and has to send me instead.'

Drake had turned to look at her and was studying her face, taking in the seriousness of her blue eyes, the tilt of confidence and determination to her chin. Slowly he said, 'I can understand his concern. You give off an aura of—' he sought for the right word '—of fragility. You remind me of one of those modern figurines. Dressed in the latest fashion but with a delicacy that is becoming lost in the contemporary world. You look as if you might easily break.'

Allie sighed, knowing exactly what he meant; her lack of height and her fine bone structure were the bane of her life—of her professional and working life, at least; in her social life they were definite assets. Firmly, she said, 'That impression is entirely wrong. It's an anachronism. I'm a professional career woman and I can handle any situation I come up against. I don't need a nursemaid, and I certainly don't need a chaperon—of either sex.'

His eyebrows lifted. 'That was a very definite statement.'

'It was meant to be.'

'And what exactly does not needing a chaperon mean?'

Steadily, her eyes holding his, she said, 'It means that I'm not a girl. I'm an experienced woman, and if I want to get friendly with someone, then I'll go ahead and do it, whether—my boss likes it or not.' She had almost said 'whether *you* like it or not', but stopped herself in time. She wanted to keep this as impersonal as possible.

But Drake had guessed and his face hardened. 'I'm beginning to think Bob is right about you,' he said shortly.

'What do you mean?'

'"The lady doth protest too much",' he quoted. Opening the car door, he said, 'Come on, let's go and eat.'

The restaurant was already quite full. It was almost impossible to tell the nationality of the customers from their dress because all looked smart; it was only as you walked by and listened to the language in which they spoke that you could tell. And everyone seemed to be talking as they ate and drank. On a small raised platform behind an equally small dance floor there was a gypsy band which was doing its best to drown out the noise of the voices.

Allie looked back over her shoulder as she turned a laughing face to Drake. 'Is it always like this?'

He seemed to draw in his breath and gazed at her for a moment before he blinked and bent nearer to hear. She repeated her question and he nodded. 'Wherever there are Russians you have noise.'

They sat down at a table for two at the rear of the room where an open window gave a welcome coolness. A waiter handed them menus but Drake didn't look at his for a few minutes. His eyes were still on Allie but there was a frowning, abstracted look in them, as if he was thinking of something quite different.

'A rouble for them,' Allie said, her eyebrows rising.

He blinked, looked disconcerted for a moment, then said hastily, 'What would you like to drink?'

They settled for vodka on the rocks and drank it while Drake explained the menu to her. 'Everyone has *zakuski*,' he told her. 'That's the same as hors d'oeuvres. And the Russians can make them last for a couple of hours. That's mostly why westerners complain about the slow service here; they eat the *zakuski* and expect the main course to be served straight away, but you have to prolong the experience.'

'Make a meal of it, you mean,' Allie said, tongue in cheek.

Drake groaned, laughed. 'I asked for that one, didn't I?'

'You didn't take up my offer,' Allie told him.

'Offer?'

'A rouble for your thoughts,' she reminded him. 'You were miles away just now.'

He gave a short laugh, said, 'Was I?' in a terse, 'leave it' kind of voice.

But Allie wasn't to be put down. 'So where were you?' she demanded.

Picking up his glass, Drake looked down at it as he gave a small shrug. 'It was nothing. For a second you reminded me of someone, that's all.'

'Oh? Who?'

'No one you'd know,' he said dismissively. 'Now, have you decided what you would like to eat?'

'Well, as I'm in Russia, I'll guess I'll go for something really authentic and have the beef stroganoff.'

That made him grin. 'Very adventurous!' he mocked.

Allie smiled back at him, wondering who it was she'd reminded him of. What woman could it have been, and what must she have meant to him to drag his mind away from the present and bring such a frown of memory to his face? 'I take it you didn't bring your family with you to Moscow,' she said lightly.

'My family?' He gave her an assessing look at the question, probably wondering if it meant she was interested in him. 'I have no family. I'm not married,' he said, his tone a little abrupt.

She nodded. 'That figures. Companies tend to send single people on foreign assignments. It's cheaper.'

'Yes, I suppose so.'

He looked slightly amused for a moment but turned to give the waiter his attention. He ordered in fluent Russian that produced the hors d'oeuvres and a bottle of Russian champagne. The gypsy band was playing away with great vigour and soon people got up to dance. Allie watched the different interpretations of the music with amusement; some tried to waltz, others to do a Highland fling, while other dancers just jigged around. The dancers were more entertaining than the band, but everyone seemed to be having a good time.

Watching her, Drake said, 'Want to try?'

'To that?' She gave him a horrified look. 'No way; I haven't had nearly enough to drink to let my hair down to that extent.'

'A slower one, then.' He beckoned a waiter over and gave him some money which was taken over to the band leader, a man with dark hair and a luxuriant moustache who obviously thought he was the bee's knees in his flamboyant costume.

The money had the desired effect and the band began to play a slow, haunting melody that could only have been a love song in any language. Drake stood and offered his hand. Hiding her reluctance, Allie let him help her to her feet and went into his arms to dance. As they moved around the room she thought how strange it was that you could be with a virtual stranger and never want or expect to be close to him, but with just the excuse of some music he could hold you as close as this, your bodies touching almost intimately, your faces, your mouths just a few inches apart. He could put his arm low on your waist, bend his head to take in the scent of your perfume, could look into your eyes and give a slow smile of awareness. An awareness that you were man and woman, that the business connection was just a superficial nonsense, a masquerade when set against the deeper, primitive sexual consciousness.

She found the thought disturbing, just as she found Drake's nearness getting to her. He moved well and held her firmly; she could feel the muscle in his arm beneath her hand, and could only guess at his strength. He was too tall for her, of course, but her high heels had lifted her close enough for Allie to get the tang of his aftershave, to be able to study the strong line of his jaw and the firmness of his lips. There was nothing full or heavy about his features and there never would be; he was all lean planes and angles, western handsomeness personified.

She began to wonder if he was very experienced with women. He didn't give off an obvious aura of knowledge, hadn't looked her over stripping her as he did so, as some men did, wondering what she would be like in bed and how much effort might have to be put into getting her there. But there was a certain class of man who was so self-confident, so assured in his own masculinity, that he didn't have to flaunt his experience. And that type of man was far more attractive to a woman than the more obvious kind.

Was Drake that kind of man? Allie wondered. A rather boisterous pair of dancers pushed towards them and Drake pulled her close and swung her out of the way. She followed him effortlessly, their steps perfectly matched, then laughed up at him. 'That was close.'

'Mmm.' He looked down at her musingly for a moment and she wondered if he could guess what she was thinking about him.

Mischievously, she said, 'You're miles away again. Where are you this time?'

She wasn't sure what to expect, but it certainly wasn't for him to say, completely out of the blue, 'I know you have an ulterior motive in coming to Russia.'

She came to a precipitate stop, too disconcerted to be able to prevent her face filling with horrified dismay as she stared at him in appalled consternation. How could he know? How could he possibly have found out?

CHAPTER TWO

SOMEBODY bumped into her and Allie hastily moved out of the way, lowering her face, trying to hide her consternation. But her mind was screaming in mingled fright and anger. Who had told him? How could he possibly know? The two, oh, so *vital* questions burned into her brain. With a supreme effort she somehow lifted her head to look at Drake, forcing an amused smile to her mouth. Her voice sounding odd even to her own ears, she managed to say lightly, 'What on earth gives you that idea?'

She hadn't fooled him for a minute. Drake was gazing down at her with a frown of incredulous surprise in his grey eyes, and she could almost hear his brain computing her reaction, trying to work out why such a simple remark had disconcerted her so much. 'It was something Bob said.'

It was such a deliberately ambiguous reply that she felt a spurt of anger but managed to fight it down, aware that he was watching her, studying her face. But she couldn't understand how Bob could possibly know; she'd told no one, it was a secret she'd shared with only one person in the world—and she had been dead for years now. Fighting for normality, for lightness, Allie said, 'Really? I can't think what it was. What did he say, exactly?'

The direct question had pushed him into a corner

and Allie knew that he would have to give her a direct answer, but the wretched man side-stepped again by saying, 'He mentioned that you had an—outside interest in Russia.'

At any other time she might have enjoyed this verbal fencing, but this issue was much too important, made her too anxious to want to prolong it. And it was such dangerous ground. She gave a small shrug, pretending indifference. 'I can't think what he means.'

It left the opening up to Drake; he could come right out with it or he could go on playing cat and mouse with her. Allie kept her expression casual, as if nothing was the matter, even looking round the room and humming to the music.

She didn't know whether she'd managed to deceive him or not, but she felt his eyes still fixed on her when he said, 'Bob told me that you've already written a couple of books for children and would probably use this visit to get background for another.'

So that was it! Allie felt a huge wave of intense relief run through her, her legs felt as if they wanted to sag and her shoulders sank as the tightness left them. But she did her best to hide it by giving an embarrassed laugh. 'Oh, that!'

'What else could he have meant?' The question showed that Drake hadn't been taken in for a minute. He was holding her quite close and must have felt the sudden loss of tension.

Ignoring the question, she glanced up at him from under her lashes, still pretending to be embarrassed. 'I'd hoped Bob had forgotten all about my writing. He teased me about it unmercifully when he first found out. Called me the future Enid Blyton of the twenty-first century. Thought it was a great joke. You know what he's like.'

'Does that worry you?'

The music came to an end and Allie stepped away from him, lifted an arm to push her hair off her forehead as they walked back to their table. 'Here I am, busy projecting myself as a successful career woman, a go-ahead jet-setter with the lifestyle to go with it. Writing stories for young children hardly fits the image.'

His voice dry, Drake said, 'And is your image that important to you?'

Of course it darn well mattered, she thought in annoyance. Where the hell had he been if he thought that the image a person projected wasn't all-important in their career, their chances of promotion? 'Isn't yours?' she countered.

'What one does is surely more important than the way one looks while you're doing it.'

'Actions speak louder than appearances, in other words,' Allie said wryly.

His eyebrows rising at her tone, Drake said, 'You sound as if you don't believe it.'

'I can't afford to. You may not have noticed, but I'm a woman.'

Drake had been about to take a drink but stopped at that, his eyes widening. With a sudden and rather surprising smile, he said, 'Er—yes, I had noticed, as a matter of fact.'

'Women have to be far more image-conscious than men.'

'Isn't that attitude rather dated?' he asked on a cautious note.

He was right to be cautious; Allie could easily have snapped his head off. What could he, a jumped-up bank clerk, possibly know about the fight that women with any ambition had on their hands the minute they entered the business world? To succeed they not only had to be as good as men but better, and they had to look good, too. Power-dressing was exactly what it implied—a physical projection of where they wanted to be, the path they wanted to tread.

A man could turn up for work in yesterday's shirt, his suit crumpled, and his contemporaries immediately thought that he'd had a night on the tiles and admired him for it. If a woman turned up looking at all unkempt her male colleagues would think she was sleeping around and treat her accordingly, while her female workmates would probably think she had given up the uneven struggle and was letting herself go.

Inwardly at zero tolerance level, Allie just gave Drake a sweet smile and said, 'No—but yours is.'

He looked taken aback and his eyes narrowed. Leaning forward, he looked as if he was going to argue, but thankfully the cabaret started, dancers dressed in vivid, exotic costumes springing onto the dance floor. The music became high and heated and it was impossible to talk. Allie turned her chair slightly to watch, her face averted, presenting only the fine line of her profile to Drake's gaze. When the sweating dancers finished their performance, the waiter hurried to bring their main course, and when he had gone Allie made sure to turn the conversation into safer channels.

It was a prolonged meal and she didn't enjoy it. She realised that her reaction to Drake's remark about her having an ulterior motive in coming to Russia, which he'd made in all innocence, had aroused his curiosity. He was watchful now, scenting a mystery he couldn't fathom. As soon as he got home he would probably be on the phone to her boss, trying to solve it, she thought with chagrin, angry at herself for having given so much away. But the remark had taken her completely by surprise, there had been no warning, no few precious moments in which to prepare herself for it.

'Tell me how you came to write the story books,' he invited.

'I have a little god-daughter. I was baby-sitting one night when she couldn't sleep, so I made up a story. But she's a very modern child, everything has to be visual, so I had to draw pictures of the characters for her. Her father saw them and suggested I try to get it published.' She shrugged. 'No big deal at all, really.'

'Did they sell well?'

'Quite well,' Allie admitted, with an inner surge of pleasure at the thought of her success. 'But not well enough to give up the day job,' she added firmly, in case he passed that piece of information on to her boss.

But Drake disarmed her by grinning as he said, 'I'm sure Bob would be pleased to hear you say that. He told me that you're a great asset to his company.'

'He did?' Allie's eyes widened. Her boss wasn't

exactly generous with praise and compliments. The most she usually got from him was, 'Not bad. Not bad, considering.'

'I'm sure he wouldn't want to lose you,' Drake said in some amusement, as if reading her mind.

She didn't like it when his mouth twisted into that amused smile; it was condescending, as if she were just some dumb female, not to be taken seriously. It put her back up.

'How sweet of you to reassure me. And where will you be based when you leave Russia?' she asked him. 'Back in London—or do you just dutifully go wherever you're sent?'

The edge of sarcasm in her tone wasn't lost on him. Drake's eyes narrowed, but he admitted, 'I go where I'm needed. But isn't that what you do?'

She gave one of her sudden, impish and completely natural smiles. *'Touché.'* His eyes came swiftly to her face with an arrested expression, but before he could speak Allie pretended to stifle a yawn. 'It's been quite a long day. Would you mind taking me back to my hotel?'

'Of course. You must be tired after your journey.'

She wasn't; Allie had seldom felt more inwardly alert as they drove back to the city centre, but she lay back against her seat, letting him think her exhausted.

When they reached her hotel, she turned to thank him for the evening, but Drake said, 'I'll see you inside.' And, opening the passenger door of the car, he escorted her into the entrance.

There she turned and offered her hand, gave him a practised smile. 'Thank you so much for a wonderful evening. It was a perfect start to my stay here. And thank you again for meeting me and everything. I'll be sure to tell Bob how kind you've been.'

There was dismissal in every sentence, distance in her smile. Drake took her hand but not the dismissal. Instead he said, 'It was my pleasure. I know you'll be working during the day, but have you any thoughts on where you would like to go tomorrow evening?'

'That's very kind of you, but I expect I'll be busy working out my shooting schedule, that kind of thing,' she responded easily.

'That's a shame. The ballet are performing tomorrow and I'm sure I could manage to get a couple of tickets.'

'The ballet? Russian ballet?' Allie was immediately torn; seeing the ballet performed here in Russia was a lifelong ambition. Well, she'd intended to see it some time while she was here, so why not let Drake take her? So she smiled and said, 'You've found my weakness. I couldn't possibly refuse a chance like that.'

'Good. I'll meet you here at seven tomorrow, then.' And only then did he let go of her hand.

Allie smiled. 'Thanks again. Goodnight.' She turned and walked across the deep foyer to the lifts, joined a small group of waiting people. When the lift came she glanced back. Drake was still there, hands hooked into the pockets of his trousers, watching her. She lifted her hand in a small wave goodbye and walked into the lift.

As Drake watched her walk away from him his thoughts were on her legs. Although she was so petite her figure was perfect and her legs very shapely, with the kind of slim ankles that he liked on a woman. There were other tourists, women among them, waiting for the lift and he was sure she would be quite safe, but he stayed where he was. When Allie waved, he merely nodded, and waited until the lift doors had closed before going back to the car.

He was fully aware that she didn't want him around; Bob had warned him that she was an independently minded girl. What he hadn't been warned about was her attractiveness, her air of fragility that immediately appealed to his protective instincts. Fleetingly he wondered if Bob, who knew everything about his past, had deliberately brought them together for reasons other than that of convenience. But he pushed that thought aside. What intrigued him now was that moment of open fear Allie had shown earlier. If her secondary reason in coming to Russia had been merely to write a children's book, why be so frightened that he should know? No, there had to be something more than that. Something that Bob Delaney didn't know about.

Drake negotiated the streets and pulled into the garage below his apartment building, pondering the problem. Had she perhaps undertaken to carry out an assignment for some other organisation at the same time as Bob's? Working for two companies without telling her employer? It was possible, he supposed. From only spending one evening with her he was aware that Allie was very ambitious. If she thought it might help her career she might well agree to take on the extra

work, even though she probably knew that Bob
wouldn't approve.

Maybe she was even lining up to move on to another company, or to start up as a freelance. So perhaps it was the fact that she was deceiving Bob, who
was his friend, that had made her so prickly towards
him, made her react so guiltily. Whatever it was, he
would do his best to discover it, Drake decided. After
all, Bob had been a good friend to his parents, and to
him when he'd most needed one; he owed it to him
to find out.

But as he entered his flat and moved over to the
window to look out over the lights of the city in the
direction of her hotel Drake knew that that was just a
feeble excuse; the truth was that he was intrigued by
Allie herself and couldn't resist getting to know her
better. But whether that was wise, in view of his own
past and even more uncertain future, was an extremely
debatable point.

Allie was eager to get down to work the next morning
but found that it was first necessary to get to know
Professor Martos and his assistants. She was given a
tour round the whole museum, which was fascinating,
but her mind was entirely on the Fabergé eggs which
she was shown last. The professor took her to the
display case but stood with his back to it as he gave
her a lecture on Fabergé and his factory, before at last
moving out of the way, indicating the eggs with a
flourish of his arm, like a conjuror waving his wand.

Allie gasped, and stared. The treasure that he'd re-
vealed was the cream of an Aladdin's cave. Gold, sil-

ver, the flash of diamonds and rubies, the gleam of
platinum and crystal—all these were there, but those
were mundane in comparison to the fantastic work-
manship in which they were contained. There were
ten eggs in all, arranged on two shelves of the large
cabinet. Some of them were large, some small in comparison, but all were different. And most of them had
a hidden surprise.

One of them was a clock crowned with a delicate
bouquet of lilies carved from onyx, another had a
scale working model of a Trans-Siberian railway train
that folded to fit inside, the tiny key that wound the
mechanism lying beside it. A third was a music box,
and others contained miniature portraits of the
Imperial family, their young faces smiling confidently
into the future they would never see. A small replica
of the royal yacht floated on a crystal sea, another egg
opened to show a painting in a golden frame.

Her eyes wide with wonder and pleasure, Allie
gazed at the eggs, the Easter gifts of the last Tsar of
Russia to his wife and his mother. Last of all, she
allowed her gaze to move to one of the smallest eggs.
It was covered in clover leaves of transparent, bright
green enamel, their shapes outlined by gold threads.
Here and there between the foliage wound a thin
golden ribbon paved with rubies. Although one of the
smallest examples it was also one of the most attractive, a masterpiece of the jeweller's art.

'Doesn't that egg have a surprise inside?' she
asked, pointing to it.

Professor Martos raised his hands in a helpless gesture and said, with his heavy accent, 'Alas, it has been

lost. But records show that it once had four leaves set inside it, each with a portrait of the emperor's daughters, and was set with twenty-three perfect diamonds.'

'What a shame,' Allie murmured, and hid her excitement by immediately pointing to a different egg and asking questions about it.

The professor was pleased to air his knowledge and practise his English, and they got down to fixing shooting schedules. It was arranged that they would photograph one egg per day with a break for Sunday. The eggs were to be taken from the show cabinet to a special room, but Allie wasn't to be allowed to handle them, she was warned; the professor and his assistants would do that. But he promised he would give her all the help she needed for the very handsome fee that her company was paying the museum. She was shown the room where the shoot was to take place; it was adequate, about thirty feet square, windowless, and with the walls painted white to reflect the light. 'I will want to take one film of all the eggs together,' she warned.

Allie took a loose-leaf binder from her document case and showed Professor Martos the outline that she envisaged for the CD-ROM. 'We'll need a wide shot of all the eggs so that people can click on to the one they want to go to,' she explained.

'It will have to be done at night, or when the museum is closed,' he told her.

They were discussing arrangements when footsteps sounded in the empty gallery. Allie thought it was the tourists entering for the next visiting period, but when she glanced round she saw only one man—Sergei Morozov.

He shook hands first with the professor and then with her, holding her hand longer than was necessary as he told the professor how they had already met. 'You have already seen round the museum? That is a shame; I had promised myself that pleasure. As you've already seen the Armoury perhaps you would let me show you round some other museums instead?'

Allie sensed that the professor wasn't too happy about having Sergei hanging around, so she said, 'Having seen these wonderful eggs, it looks as if I'm going to be very busy, but perhaps I could give you a ring when I have some free time.'

'"Give me a...?" Oh, you mean call, telephone. I understand. But it will be easier for me to call your hotel, I think.' He turned to the professor, said something in Russian to which the older man shook his head, then glanced at his watch and said a time. One o'clock. The phrase was easy enough for Allie to understand it.

When he'd gone they finalised arrangements for the day on which all the eggs were to be photographed together, everyone agreeing that early the following Sunday morning would be best. An hour or so later Allie left the museum, walking out of its cool atmosphere into the midday heat. She paused to put on her dark glasses and wasn't at all surprised to see Sergei leaning on the railing outside, waiting for her.

Straightening, he came forward and said with an easy smile, 'I remembered that I have to go to a very famous monastery not far from Moscow this afternoon. To check on the building, you understand. And I thought, on such a beautiful day, what could be better than to show this most beautiful place to our most beautiful tourist?'

Allie wrinkled her nose at him. 'Sergei, that is the corniest line I ever heard.'

He laughed. 'But it is what they say in the movies all the time.'

'You must watch some very old movies.'

He laughed again, not in the least put out. 'But you will come with me, yes?'

'Where is this place?'

'At Zagorsk. It is the biggest monastery in Russia as well as being the most beautiful. Everyone goes there. You must not miss it.'

She had heard of the place, of course, not only from her reading about Russia in preparation for this trip, but in tales told long ago. And she'd had every intention of going there, so if Sergei wanted to take her—well, why not? 'Sure. I'd like to.'

Rewarding her decision with a delighted smile, Sergei led her out of the Kremlin, saying, 'My car is just a short distance away.'

As they walked along, the sun rippling on the surface of the River Moskva on their left, Allie remembered Drake's warning about getting too friendly. She smiled inwardly, quietly confident of her ability to handle Sergei if the need arose. But then the forcefulness in Drake's voice came back to her; maybe it wouldn't do any harm to be cautious. So when they reached Sergei's car, a well-polished but old German

model, she said, 'I'll have to go back to my hotel first;
I can't visit a monastery dressed like this.'

He tried to demur but she insisted, and while in her
room she wrote down where she was going and with
whom, leaving the note with the receptionist to give
to Drake if he should ask for her.

As it turned out the precaution was completely un-
necessary. Sergei drove the seventy kilometres or so
to Zagorsk, telling her something of his life in Russia
but far more interested in life in London.

'Haven't you ever been there?' she asked him.

'For one week only, to study the architecture. It
rained all the time.'

Allie laughed. 'It does tend to do that.'

'But I have been to America,' Sergei told her. 'Now
that is an amazing country. I studied English and
architecture there for nearly two years.'

'I thought your English had an American accent.'

'It does? I did not realise that.'

The monastery was everything Sergei had promised. Its buildings covered a vast area and it came
complete with onion domes in gold, and brilliant blue
encrusted with gold stars, with towers and steeples,
with an uncountable number of religious buildings,
and even a museum full of beautiful icons.

Being with Sergei was definitely a help; where the
way into a church was barred to ordinary tourists, he
merely spoke a few words to the robed and bearded
priest who guarded the entrance and they were allowed inside. Allie had changed into an ankle-length
skirt and a long-sleeved blouse back at the hotel and
had covered her hair with a lightweight scarf as they'd

entered the monastery, so she didn't stand out too much from the crowds of worshippers who packed all the shrines and churches. All of these were breath-taking; richly adorned, their walls of painted icons, most of them overlaid in gold or silver, reflected the sunlight. There were no seats inside these holy places; in the Russian orthodox church everyone stood, murmuring their prayers.

Her only regret was that she wasn't alone, but without Sergei she probably wouldn't have been allowed inside these sacred places. He stood quite close beside her, but Allie shut her eyes and tried to forget him, to lose herself in the atmosphere of veneration around her. It must have been like this for hundreds of years, she thought, for all the ancestors who had lived in Russia so long ago. They must have stood in churches just like this, prayed as these people were praying, worshipped in exactly the same way. She tried to feel as they must have felt, but it was all too strange, too alien to her upbringing, to the modern western woman that she had become.

Outside again, they wandered around.

'Didn't you come here to do some work?' Allie asked after a while.

Sergei gave her a bland smile. 'But that is what I'm doing as we walk around.'

Allie laughed as she was meant to. 'It's very kind of you to show me round like this, but I wouldn't want you to neglect your work.'

'It's my pleasure. But you have seen very little as yet. There is much of Moscow still to see.' He hesitated for a moment, then said, 'And you must try some typical Russian food. Perhaps you would let me take you to a restaurant I know tonight?'

'How nice of you to ask me, but Drake Marsden has already invited me out.'

'That's a great shame. Perhaps—'

'Some other time? Of course. Although I'm going to be rather busy with my work, of course. Oh, look at that amazing tower!' she exclaimed as they turned a corner. 'How old is it, do you know?'

Her ploy to change the subject worked and they talked Russian history until it was time to leave. Sergei drove her back to Moscow but they got snarled up in the traffic and it was quite late before he dropped her off at the hotel. Allie cursed a little as she hurried to change; this was probably the only time she would ever get to go to the ballet at the Bolshoi and she wanted to look good for the occasion. As she sorted through her wardrobe for something suitable to wear Allie remembered Drake's comment about her look of fragility and pouted a little. If he thought she didn't look capable of taking care of herself it was going to be even harder to get rid of him. So maybe it wouldn't do any harm to show him another side of her persona. Smiling, she took out her red dress.

After washing her hair, Allie drew it smoothly back from her head but with a knot of curls at the nape, fastened with jewelled clips. The red dress wasn't *really* all that revealing, at least when viewed from the front. It was when she turned round that the perspective changed. The front had a high halter neck, but was completely bare at the back. The skirt was long, but had two slits up the sides that reached to her thighs. And it clung so sleekly that it was quite impossible to wear anything underneath it. Adding a pair of red suede wedge shoes, Allie slung a small evening bag on her shoulder, laughed at her reflection in the mirror, and went down to give Drake ample opportunity to revise his first impression of her.

It had the desired effect—and some. But Allie hadn't been quite prepared for the effect that Drake, in immaculate evening dress, would have on her. Too impatient to wait for the lift, she ran lightly down the wide staircase, but paused when she reached the mezzanine floor to glance down over the balcony rail. She could see Drake in profile, glancing up at the clock above the reception desk, his features sharp, his chin with a determined thrust to it. The lift reached the ground floor and he turned to see if she was in it. It was then that she suddenly realised that she fancied him. Perhaps it was the elegance of his clothes, the air of complete self-assurance that they gave him. Whatever it was, Allie felt a surge of pleasure at the sight of him. They would look good together, she thought. She would enjoy being seen with him. Her eyes became contemplative; maybe it would be fun to make him fall for her after all.

Allie continued to watch him for several minutes, trying to resist the temptation, knowing that at best it would be foolish, at worst almost dangerous, bearing in mind her real reason for coming to Russia. But there was something challenging about him; she had the feeling that he could be extremely sexy under that cool, almost aloof exterior. Confident of her own attractiveness to the male sex, Allie had no real doubt that she could make him fall for her if she put her mind to it. She ought not to, of course, but the major question was, did she really want to? Drake again looked at the clock, then shoved his hands in his pockets in an impatient movement.

It was that one gesture that decided her. Allie resolved to make him so crazy about her that he would do anything for her, be so eager to see her that he would willingly wait hours for her if necessary. And for a start she was determined that he would kiss her before the evening was out. Drawing back from the balcony, she walked round to the lifts and punched the button, preferring to use the elevator rather than push through a crowd of tourists who were climbing the stairs.

In tacit agreement the other people in the lift stood aside for her to leave first, probably to get a better look at her back view. Allie ought to have politely thanked them, but she just walked across the foyer towards Drake, liking the way his eyes had widened at sight of her. That her dress was causing quite a sensation among the other guests she chose to ignore.

When she reached him, he gave a slow smile and said, 'I feel as if a hidden orchestra somewhere ought to be playing "Lady in Red".' She laughed and he said, 'You're late again,' but now he no longer seemed to mind so much.

Drake went to put an arm behind her, to shepherd her to the door, felt her bare flesh and stepped back a pace. Allie heard the sharp intake of his breath and glanced over her shoulder, the impish smile playing on her mouth. She expected to see not only surprise but awareness in his eyes, and for a moment it was there, but then a grim look came into his face. 'Do you have a coat or something?'

'No!' She gave a laugh of incredulous surprise. 'Of course not. It's much too warm.'

His mouth tightened, and for a horrid moment she thought he was going to order her to go back to her room and get one. Good grief! Was the man a prude? He seemed to hesitate, but must have seen the stubborn lift to her chin because he then strode forward and opened the entrance door for her, his face set.

Drake didn't speak until they were in the waiting car, and then he said on a curt note, 'I think you like living dangerously.'

'Because I chose to wear this dress? Don't be ridiculous.'

'This isn't some nightclub in London that we're going to. Women dress more—circumspectly here. Not that that dress wouldn't make heads turn anywhere.'

'Look, if it upsets you that much, then let's just forget the whole thing,' Allie said angrily. 'As it is you've already ruined the evening.'

Drake glanced at her, pushed his hair back from his forehead and swore softly under his breath. Then said, 'I'm sorry.' Starting the car, he pulled out into the street.

Never had Allie so swiftly regretted a decision; the man was just an insufferable prig. Any other man would have been knocked out by her dress, would have enjoyed being with a woman who attracted so many envious eyes. They sat in grim silence until they reached Sverdlov Square, parked, and walked through the white-columned portico of the theatre. Drake bought her a programme and she had to thank him, but she let him know by the tilt of her chin that he was still in the doghouse, and her anger increased when he hurried her to her seat—to hide her bare back, she supposed.

But when the ballet started she forgot their argument and become lost in the magic of the performance. It was *Coppelia* and she loved the colourful costumes, the realistic set of the country village, and the brilliant skill of the dancers. When the first interval came round she gave a sigh of pure contentment. 'I don't think I've ever seen it danced so well. All the dancers are incredibly good.'

'You go to the ballet a lot?' Drake asked.

'Whenever I can. I had ambitions to be a dancer when I was young,' she confided.

Drake's eyebrow rose. 'You have the perfect figure for it. What made you give it up?'

She gave a small shrug. 'I was in an accident and broke my leg quite badly. It took a long while to heal and I lost out on too many lessons and practice. I was never able to make it up, and I eventually realised that I would only ever be second-rate.' She paused, her voice wistful, before saying, 'So I gave it up. I concentrated on art and photography instead.'

'What sort of accident? A car smash?'

'No. I fell off a horse,' Allie said with a little grimace.

'It must have been a great disappointment for you.'

'It was at the time, but maybe I would never have

been better than second-rate anyway. Who knows? Maybe it did me a favour.'

'I hardly think having your hopes and ambitions dashed, your life blighted—however temporarily—can be called a favour,' Drake pointed out.

His voice was curt, almost accusing, and she gave him a quick glance, wondering what the hell it was with him. One minute he seemed perfectly ordinary, the next he was acting like some stern schoolmaster, and taking the most innocent remark almost as if she had deliberately set out to annoy him on a personal level.

Allie fanned herself with her programme. 'It's very warm—could we have a drink?'

'You sure you wouldn't prefer me to get you an ice-cream?'

'No, I'd much rather a drink.'

Drake sighed and got to his feet. 'Come on, then.'

The bar was packed and there was nowhere to sit, so Allie stood as near to the open window as she could get while Drake fought his way through the throng at the bar. The audience seemed to be on the young side and was quite well-dressed, but the women's clothes were more conventional than in Europe or the States, Allie had to admit. It didn't particularly worry her, but she stood with her back to the wall all the same.

There was one more interval in the performance but Allie didn't ask to go for another drink, instead content to spend the time looking round the huge auditorium with its richly ornate decoration and twisting her neck to admire the painted ceiling. When the dancers took their final bows at the end, the curtains closed and the great chandelier above them again blazed with light, Allie gave a sigh and turned to Drake with a smile of genuine gratitude. 'That was wonderful. Thank you.'

She found him watching her with a curiously bleak look, his eyes expressive not of sorrow exactly, but of regret.

'What is it?' she asked curiously.

'What? Oh, nothing.' He stood abruptly. 'Let's get out of here.'

Drake was close behind her as they stood in the slowly moving crowd of people making for the exits, but once outside they found a summer storm had blown up and it had started to rain heavily. The road fronting the theatre was already thick with cars and taxis jockeying to get to the kerb.

'We'll have to make a dash for the car,' Drake said, looking out at the rain.

'No, I'll wait here while you go and get it.'

'I can't leave you here alone.'

'Oh, rubbish!' Allie exclaimed, starting to get annoyed again. 'I'll be perfectly all right among all these people. I'll get soaked otherwise.'

Drake looked as if he was going to argue, but just then there was a crack of thunder and the rain began to really pelt down. He glanced round, saw that there were several other women waiting, and nodded reluctantly. 'OK. I'll be as quick as I can. Don't talk to anyone.' And, turning up the collar of his jacket, he sprinted down the road towards the car.

He must have found it difficult to get the car into

the traffic stream because he was gone for some time. A couple of other cars and taxis pushed their way to the kerb and picked up people; other people put up umbrellas and made a run for the nearest Metro station, until there were few left. There were two men standing together nearby, middle-aged, quite prosperous-looking. One of them came up, spoke to her, asked her if she was waiting for someone. Allie understood the question but pretended ignorance, shrugging her shoulders.

She took a couple of steps away, looking out into the street for the car, but the man followed her and was joined by his friend. One put his hand on her arm and stroked it, said something that needed no translation in any language. Allie gave him a fiery look and thought of going back into the theatre, but the doors had closed, the lights were being turned out. She shook him off, trying to ignore him. But he wouldn't be ignored, putting his hand on her back this time. Allie clutched her handbag and prepared to hit him with it, but just then there was a terrific squealing of brakes and blaring of horns as a car cut straight across the traffic lanes and swerved to a stop beside her. Drake was out of the car almost before it had stopped. With an outraged snarl, he said something to the man that made him drop his hand as if he'd been scalded, then opened the passenger door for Allie and almost shoved her inside.

'I thought I told you not to talk to anyone!' Drake exclaimed furiously as soon as he joined her.

'I didn't. He spoke to me,' she retorted, pleased that

he'd come along, but darned if she was going to let him read her a lecture.

'I knew it was a mistake to let you wear that damn dress; I should have made you go and change.'

Allie gave a gasp of anger. So much for trying to turn him on; all he'd done all evening was go off at her. 'What's the matter with you?' she flared at him, angry that her scheme had backfired. 'You're not my keeper. I'll wear what I damn well like. Stop the car!'

'What?' He gave her a startled glance.

'You heard me. Stop the car. I've had enough of you.'

'If you think I'm going to let you walk through the middle of Moscow alone at night, then you're crazy. Especially dressed in that thing.'

'"Thing"! I'll have you know this dress cost a small fortune.'

'You were robbed.'

At any other time that remark would have appealed to her sense of humour, but Allie was so mad at having her evening ruined that she yelled, 'If you don't stop this car I'll put my head out of the window and start screaming. I'll tell everyone you're kidnapping me,' she threatened.

Drake laughed. 'Go ahead. No one will understand a word you're saying.'

Furious, Allie groped for the electric window catch, found it and leaned out of the window, opened her mouth to start yelling.

There wasn't any dress he could get hold of to pull her back in so, with a curse, Drake pulled into the side and stopped. Only then did he catch hold of her wrist as she started to get out of the car. 'You're not going anywhere. Look, I—'

Allie immediately began to scream.

There was only one thing to be done. Leaning forward, Drake pulled her towards him and covered her mouth with his.

It wasn't a kiss. They were both furious. 'You crazy little idiot!' Drake muttered against her lips. 'What the hell are you trying to do?'

'How dare you tell me what I should or shouldn't wear?' she raged back at him.

'Anyone with any sense would have—' He was still speaking against her mouth, but stopped abruptly, realising the incongruity of what they were doing.

It made Allie see how ridiculous it was too. For a moment she was still, but then felt a quiver run through him, not of awareness but of mirth. She lifted her head, eyes wide, to look at him and suddenly they both collapsed with laughter.

'God, what a pair of idiots,' Drake chuckled.

Allie had her hands on his shoulders where she'd been trying to push him away and after a moment she lifted one hand to touch his neck gently. 'Thanks for coming to my rescue,' she said huskily. 'It was such a wonderful evening, too.'

His eyes dwelt on her face, her long eyelashes casting shadows on her cheeks. 'Yes, it was,' he agreed softly. He moved to draw near to her again, as if he was really going to kiss her this time. She smelt the woody muskiness of his aftershave, felt a stirring of excited anticipation deep inside. But then Drake gave a crooked kind of grin and straightened, pushing his hair off his forehead. 'I'd better get you home before that dress does even more damage.'

He didn't say what he meant; he didn't have to. But it was interesting that he'd said it at all.

After he'd seen her safely into her hotel and Allie was going up in the lift, she realised that in a way he had indeed kissed her that night. She had won the bet with herself, even though in the most bizarre way. It was only a game, of course, nothing at all serious. But strangely she was left with a feeling of dissatisfaction that was very close to frustration.

CHAPTER THREE

FOR the next week or so Allie concentrated hard on her work. Early every morning she went to the Armoury museum, would indicate which egg she wanted to work on, and watch Professor Martos remove it from the display case, his hands encased in white silk gloves. Escorted by an armed guard, he would carry it into the work room and set it up for Allie to photograph. It wasn't as simple as that, of course; the lights had to be right, close-ups of each part of the egg taken, the surprise extracted and photographed. Then exact measurements were taken, the history and provenance of each item carefully noted, and finally Allie took several video films of each egg as it turned on a revolving display stand.

As Allie explained to the professor, this was to be an educational CD-ROM as well as giving people a chance to see the beauty of the eggs, so there would be video inserts, as well as a commentary which would be added later.

The work took most of the day and was made difficult because Allie wasn't allowed to touch the egg herself and had to ask one of the museum assistants to move it, none of whom could speak any English. At first the professor was always on hand to oversee the work and to act as interpreter, but then Allie began to make her requests in simple Russian and Professor

Martos, pleased to be able to carry on with his own work, would leave Allie to manage without his continuous presence, satisfying himself by just popping in occasionally to make sure everything was going well.

No one seemed to question her ability to speak a little Russian, and it was strange how quickly the language came back to her when she heard it all around. It was like a nursery rhyme or fairy-tale that had often been repeated to her in childhood but had long been forgotten, but once heard again came back with startling clarity.

On several days Sergei showed up around lunchtime. Once he brought a picnic—smoked sausage, beautifully crisp rolls, and a bottle of wine—which they ate sitting on the side of an ornamental lake in the park he drove her to, throwing crumbs to the ducks and swans that nested on the banks. He again invited her to go out with him one evening, but Allie put him off, pleading pressure of work. He was OK as a friend, she enjoyed talking to him and learning about Russia, and she was grateful for the help he'd given her, but that was her only interest in him. Maybe that was a selfish attitude but Allie couldn't help it. She was finding that the more she saw of Drake, the more deeply fascinated she became by him.

When she returned to her hotel each afternoon she would find him waiting for her and they would go out, armed with her camera, to take pictures of places connected with the Fabergé company. He had done a lot of research for her, finding shops that had sold the factory's products, houses where members of the

Fabergé family had lived, anecdotes about the eggs, that kind of thing. Allie protested a little when he brought her the first pieces of information, saying, 'This is fantastic—but I really can't let you spend so much of your time on this. It's part of *my* job.'

'Are you saying you don't want me to help?' Drake asked evenly.

'Not at all,' Allie assured him swiftly, because in fact it suited her very well. But she felt obliged to add, 'But it must be taking up a lot of your time and I'm sure you must have loads of things to do.' Then she said, because she wanted him to deny it, 'Things that you'd rather do.'

She looked at him from under her lashes as she said it, wondering about him, whether he was physically attracted to her. She was pretty sure that he was, but the annoying man was so enigmatic most of the time that she couldn't be absolutely certain. His coolness intrigued her. Especially as she knew that he was capable of deeper feelings, even if so far she had only seen his anger. She hadn't again antagonised him by wearing a revealing dress, but sometimes she tried to tease him, testing him, seeing how far she could go. And always in the back of her mind was that angry kiss he had given her and the growing need to have him repeat it, but with desire instead of anger. So far, though, he hadn't risen to any of her ploys. Rather he had seemed to see through them and would merely give one of his twisted smiles of amusement.

Seldom had she met anyone who was so reticent about himself. Most men liked nothing better than to talk about themselves, but with Drake she had learned little more about him after almost two weeks of seeing him every day than she had after the first few hours. Not that he had learned a great deal about her, either; Allie had to admit that. And not for want of try-ing—although he disguised it well, asking the most subtle questions that would lead her into a trap. It was evident that Drake still had his suspicions about her visit to Moscow. To try and fool him she would some-times pretend to have an idea and would make notes for a children's story, or go off into a dream as she saw a place that might be used in the next book.

Now he merely said, 'I'm quite enjoying it. Doing this kind of research is so different from banking.'

They were walking along a street opening off one of the boulevards that formed a horseshoe round the city, the late afternoon sun still hot on their backs. 'Do you know where you're going to be sent next?' she asked him idly.

'No. I'll decide when I get back to London.'

'Decide?' She raised her eyebrows. 'Do you get a choice, then?'

Drake gave a slight frown, perhaps of annoyance, then shrugged and said, 'There's usually expansion going on in more than one area.'

An ambiguous answer if ever she'd heard one, Allie thought, and made a mental note to ask her boss more about him when she next rang to report progress.

'How about you?' Drake was asking. 'Any idea where you're going next?'

'Oh, that's easy. I'm going to America to do some more work on this CD-ROM. There are a great many

Fabergé eggs all over the States, more than there are in Russia, in fact.'

'Where exactly?'

'There's a whole group of them in The Forbes Magazine Collection in New York, others in Washington and New Orleans. Three in the Virginia Museum of Fine Arts in Richmond, and another three in Baltimore. And other odd ones in private collections, of course.'

They found the place they were looking for on the corner of Bolshoy Kiselny Pereulok. It was an ornate eighteenth-century stone building of three storeys, once crowned by an Imperial Eagle on the roof over the entrance. It was here that the Fabergé company had opened their first shop in Moscow in 1887, and as Allie took her photos of it she could almost imagine the carriages drawing up outside and the richly dressed patrons making their purchases of the extraordinary jewellery and rich, delicate ornaments. But now the shop had long gone, along with the company, and the road was thick with cars instead of stately carriages.

To get a better shot, Allie glanced over her shoulder then stepped off the kerb into the road. A car honked angrily just as Drake pulled her back. 'But the road was clear!' she exclaimed.

'You looked the wrong way.'

'Oh, of course. I always forget that the traffic drives on the wrong side of the road here.'

'Forgetting something like that could be fatal,' he told her, his voice grim.

He was holding her quite close and Allie had to

admit that she didn't mind in the least. Tilting her head, she gave him a flirtatious smile. 'Am I to be indebted to you for ever for saving my life?'

She expected him to laugh, to perhaps make a reply in kind, as any red-blooded man would have done. But a closed look seemed to come over Drake's face and he said shortly, 'It was hardly that.'

'The car could have run me down,' she persisted. 'You saved me from a fate worse than death.'

His face suddenly went very white and Drake's hold on her arm tightened fiercely for a second before he abruptly let her go. 'What a stupid remark.' His voice was very cold, distant. 'Have you finished here? Let's go, then.'

Allie didn't move. 'Ouch!'

'What's the matter?'

'I just cut myself on that ring of ice you've put round you.'

He frowned, put up a hand to push his hair off his forehead. 'Sorry. Look, let's go and have a drink; it's too hot to walk around.'

They found a Mexican bar with tables outside and ordered long, cold Danish beers. Allie took a much needed swallow of hers then sat back to study Drake from under her lashes. He was looking away from her but must have been aware of her gaze because he said, his eyes still averted, 'Well?'

'Well what?'

'What conclusion have you come to about me?'

'Why so sure I'm thinking about you?'

He turned to look at her, reached over and took off

her sunspecs. It was like switching on a light, her vitality shining out. 'Weren't you?'

'Yes,' she admitted.

'And so?'

Allie smiled a little. 'I was wondering why you dislike me so much.'

'Dislike you!' His head jerked up. 'Of course I don't dislike you. In fact I—' He broke off abruptly.

'Don't stop there!' Allie exclaimed. 'For an unbelievable moment I thought you were going to pay me a compliment.'

An intent look came into his grey eyes. 'Oh, I could pay you all sorts of...' His voice faded and he looked away.

'Of what?' She leaned forward.

But Drake ducked the question, saying instead, 'Have I been so disagreeable?'

She studied his face, tanned from the sun, lean and handsome, and found that she couldn't say what she really felt. Instead she said stiltedly, 'Of course not. You've been very kind.'

'Oh, dear.' He gave a comical grimace. 'If that's all you can find to say, then I must have been a real pain in the butt.'

She grinned at that, but then said hesitatingly, 'Sometimes you seem very—austere.'

'Good Lord, what a terrible word. You make me sound about ninety.'

'Not at all.' Leaning forward, she put her elbow on the table and leaned her chin on it. 'Tell me about yourself,' she invited.

'What do you want to know?'

'Oh, the usual things. What are your ambitions?'

Drake gave a lopsided kind of smile. 'To go on with what I'm doing, I suppose.'

Allie frowned, having a poor opinion of that. 'But don't you want to rise within your bank? Surely you're not content to be just someone who goes around helping to open new branches?'

He gave her a quick, surprised look that changed to one of contemplation before he said, 'Someone has to do it.'

'Yes, but someone also has to be based in central office, sitting on the top of the tree and with an important share in running the company. Wouldn't you rather be that person?'

Lifting his arms, Drake linked his hands behind his head. He had taken off his jacket and the gesture stretched his shirt across his chest, outlining his muscles, creating tiny tents across the rise of his minute nipples. 'It sounds much too stressful to me,' he said lazily.

Allie had been about to tell him what she thought of such defeatism, but found that her mouth had gone dry, her chest tight, and there was a definite frisson of desire deep inside her. She wanted him! Wanted him badly. The realisation took her by surprise, took her breath away, held her in suspense as the thought took hold.

'Allie?'

She lifted her eyes from his chest but too soon to hide the awareness in her face. Seeing it, recognising it, he gave a small gasp. Hastily she lowered her head again, picked up her bag and groped inside for her handkerchief, but Drake's hand came out to catch hers and hold it still.

'Allie,' he said again, but on a note of pleased discovery this time.

Her hand trembled a little under his, but she made no attempt to take it away, instead slowly lifting her head and smiling a little ruefully. She waited for him to follow it up, to take full advantage of a need that had surprised her as much as it must have surprised him. She was working out what she would say, how she would handle his proposition, but realised that the silence was lengthening, becoming much too long. Then, to her amazement, Drake took his hand away. Lifting up his glass, he emptied it and said, 'If you've finished, shall we go?'

Hardly able to believe her ears, Allie stared at him for a moment, but he wouldn't meet her eyes, a tight, closed look on his face. Slowly she got to her feet. 'Of course,' she said shortly.

They began to walk along the street, Allie keeping apart from him, striding out, silent. But after a few minutes Drake slowed and said, almost angrily, 'Look, I suppose I ought to tell—'

Deliberately cutting in, Allie pointed to a huge M sign nearby and said, 'I've heard so much about the Moscow Metro; I think I'll take a ride.'

'It will be full of commuters at this time of day,' Drake objected.

'Then it will seem just like home, won't it?' And, turning, she headed for the entrance, saying over her shoulder, 'See you around.'

But Drake was right behind her as she went into

the station and by her side as she paused inside to work out what you were supposed to do. 'You have to get tokens,' he told her. 'Over there.'

Allie thought of arguing, of saying that she wanted to be alone, but that would have been an admission that she was feeling angry at being slighted. Well, she was, of course, but pride forbade that she should make a big thing out of it, so she shrugged and said, 'OK.'

The Metro was full of people so it was impossible to hold any kind of private conversation. There was no opportunity for Drake to give an explanation, if that was what he'd been about to do. And Allie was glad of it; she found that she didn't want to hear, was no longer interested. But she couldn't think why it should have upset her so much; Drake was only another man, for heaven's sake, albeit a very attractive one. After her job here was finished she would never see him again, so why get so het up about it?

But the thought of never seeing Drake again made her feel absolutely desolate. These last two weeks had been so good, she had felt so happy and content, so full of life. She wrenched her thoughts away from that, suddenly afraid to look into her feelings too deeply. It was only sexual attraction, nothing more. Soon they would go their separate ways, Drake back to London, and she would leave to carry out her search, to keep the promise she had made so blithely all those years ago.

They got out at a few of the stations so she could admire the fantastic architecture, the platforms that were more like marble palaces, the huge chandeliers, the painted ceilings and fluorescent mosaics.

'The stations are all devoted to a different theme,'
Drake told her, leaning close to her ear to make himself heard above the noise of an incoming train. 'Pro-
letarian labour, a famous poet, the Great October
Revolution, that kind of thing.'

Allie nodded and moved away, not wanting to be
close. She got a crick in her neck from staring up-
wards and loved what she saw, but Drake said they
ought to have come at a time when there weren't so
many people around. Their conversation, what there
was of it, was stilted. Allie hardly looked at him while
they were travelling between stops and gave the architecture of the stations all her attention when they
weren't. But one train carriage was very crowded and
they had to stand very close to one another. It was
easy for Drake because he could reach the rail to hold
on but Allie was too short. She had to just stand in
the crowd, but as the train lurched she was thrown
against him and Drake put out a hand to steady her.
She tried to keep her balance, to ride with the train,
but the Moscow Metro trains had minds of their own
and jerked a lot, so that he kept his hand on her arm
and she often swayed against him, even though she
tried not to.

Allie kept her eyes lowered, but she was intensely
aware of him again, of his closeness, the warm musky
smell of his skin, the strength in the hand that held
her. Around them people got on and off the train but
she took little notice, aware only of the heightening
tension between them. She felt as if Drake was willing
her to look at him, but she knew that if she did he
would see the awareness in her eyes. He had seen it

once and scorned it, and she had too much pride to be humbled again.

So she resisted his silent will, but with each passing moment the tension between them became more intense, like an electric charge that passed between them. Her breathing became shallower, not from the heat of the train or the crush of the people, as she tried to convince herself, but from this tantalising proximity, the knowledge of his body so close to hers. Allie licked lips gone dry; her neck muscles ached from the strain of keeping her head down. She wouldn't look at him; she wouldn't!

Someone pushed against her as a great surge of people got into the compartment. She was shoved up against Drake, with no space left between them. His arm went round her, protecting her. And she couldn't resist any longer, had to look up at last. The need was there, naked in his eyes, and unashamed. A smouldering hunger that he didn't try to hide. Allie gave a small gasp and stiffened as they stared into each other's face. She felt a great glow of desire begin to burn inside her. She wanted to be kissed, yearned to have his lips take hers, wouldn't even have cared that they were in such an unlikely place, surrounded by so many people. And she wanted to touch him, too, wanted that very badly.

And it was in that moment, in that stupid place, that she realised that she was in love with him.

The train pulled into another station that must have connected to other lines. The stifling crowd was suddenly gone and there was space all round them, no longer an excuse to be close. Reluctantly Drake removed his arm and she stepped away. There was a seat and she sank into it, her legs suddenly feeling like water. She went to look at Drake again but people were pushing their way on now and standing between them, so she couldn't see him. And maybe that was just as well, because it gave her a few minutes in which to cope with this tumult of emotion, to realise that it wasn't just sexual attraction but full-blown, bell-pealing, shout-it-from-the-rooftops love.

As a teenager, she had thought herself in love before, had a couple of times been completely besotted by a boyfriend. It had been so long ago that she couldn't remember very well, but instinct told her that this was different. That this was for real. The sexual attraction was overwhelming, but with it she felt intense tenderness, a feeling that every part of her—her heart and her soul, as well as her body—was in love with him. She looked down at her hands and knew that her fingertips were in love, even every minute pore of skin and every hair on her head. She felt that from this moment she existed only for him. It was a sensation that brought intense awe, great humility. It had happened to her at last, creeping up on her unawares when she had almost given up expectation. She was in love! Really in love.

Allie peered through the crowd and by moving her head almost in front of the person next to her she finally managed to glimpse Drake. Somehow she expected him to be alight with the same miracle that had engulfed her, but he wasn't looking towards her, instead was staring at nothing, a set, almost bleak look on his face. Immediately she felt afraid, and realised with sickening clarity that if you bestowed your heart, then you left yourself wide open to hurt, that you were at your most vulnerable.

They didn't get out to look at any more stations, instead leaving the Metro at the stop nearest to her hotel. Drake didn't touch her, take her arm or anything, and he seemed frighteningly impersonal, his eyes cold. His manner came as a slap in the face, an ice-cold douche to her heart. When he'd seen her inside the hotel, Drake, his voice distant, reminded her that they were going to the circus that night.

Allie would have liked to say that she no longer wanted to go, but pride wouldn't allow it. So she smiled, if somewhat coolly, and said, 'Fine. See you later.'

But when she got into her room she threw her things down onto the bed and banged around as she took off her clothes, feeling angry and rejected, and, yes, she had to admit it, darn frustrated. She could understand that he might not feel as deeply as she did, but how dared the man just ignore her when she'd let him see that she was attracted to him? And not once, but twice. He could at least have been nice about it, not got all stiff and uptight, as if the fact that she fancied him was an insult, for God's sake! OK, so he didn't fancy her in return. But that was no big deal. Reciprocal chemistry didn't always work. But any man with halfway civilised manners didn't just— In the act of stepping into the shower Allie suddenly stood still. Every instinct told her that Drake *was* attracted to her. That whatever had held him back it hadn't been indifference. She just *knew* it.

Standing under the water, Allie thought it through. She was a good-looking girl who had no trouble in attracting men; she was experienced enough to read the signs, recognise the body language. She was sure that Drake wasn't hanging around, helping her with her work and taking her out every night just to please Bob. No friend, however close, would go to those lengths, especially if it meant being with someone they didn't particularly like. And he'd done what Bob had asked: seen her settled in Moscow and made sure that she was getting on OK with her assignment. Drake ought to have been on a plane back to London days ago. But he'd stayed on to help her, although he must have realised by now that she was quite capable of managing on her own. So why hang around—unless it was because he couldn't tear himself away?

And if that was so, then why the big freeze? He wasn't married or living with anyone, she'd found that out, and he certainly wasn't gay. So why? A broken love affair and an unwillingness to risk being hurt again, perhaps? Allie imagined all sorts of scenarios, but knew that she was just wasting her time. She should have listened to him earlier when he'd seemed about to explain, but she'd been too angry and humiliated to care.

Wiping the steam from the mirror, Allie looked at her reflection. She wasn't vain by nature and had never before let it matter if a man she'd liked hadn't returned the feeling. So what? Forget and go on. But it mattered with Drake, mattered terribly. Her future, her happiness—everything—depended on him feeling the same way about her as she did about him. But he seemed to swing from attraction to indifference, from heat to ice, and she couldn't understand it. It was a puzzle, a mystery, and she determined to find out the answer.

Allie was excited about going to the Moscow State Circus, the name giving her the expectation of something very grand, but she was disappointed when they first went into the large round building because it seemed just like any other circus ring but in a permanent home. The acts, though, were excellent. There were clowns, tightrope walkers, wonderful circus horses, a duo of trapeze artists who took her breath away, and a group of performing poodle dogs who so obviously enjoyed themselves and were so funny that she completely forgot her instinctive reaction against making animals perform and doubled up with laughter. At the end of their act she joined in the loud applause and turned a laughing face to Drake.

'Weren't they wonderful? I've never seen such...' Her voice faded as she saw that Drake's eyes weren't on the ring at all but on her. In them was a look of almost desperate need, but all mixed up with a bleakness that shouldn't have been there. 'What *is* it?' she asked, her tone forceful.

He blinked, shook his head as the next act swept into the ring. But Allie could no longer lose herself in the antics of the clowns and was glad when the artistes took their bows in the grand finale. They left the circus with the rest of the audience, Drake with a hand on her arm, always protective, and walked to the car. But he didn't take her straight back to her hotel, instead driving out of the city into the countryside, to a hill that overlooked a wooded valley with a small river flowing silver in the light of the moon.

'Shall we take a walk?' he invited. 'There's a good view from the top.'

She hesitated for only a moment. 'OK.'

Leaving the car, they strolled to the top of the ridge and saw the lights of Moscow in the distance. Drake pointed out various landmarks but then they stopped in the shadow of a tree and for a few minutes were silent. Allie could have broken it but it was Drake who had suggested this and she waited to hear what he would say. When he did speak he took her breath away.

'I want to go to bed with you,' he said abruptly.

She didn't know whether to be pleased, to be angry, what to feel. She moved away from him and after a moment said accusingly, 'You sound as if it's the last thing you want, as if your libido is ruling your head.'

He gave a short laugh. 'You're right. I've fought against this.'

She gave an incredulous gasp. 'Well, thanks. Thanks a lot!'

His eyes intent, Drake hardly heard her as he went on, 'But I can't conceal it any longer. I've wanted you from the first moment I saw you.'

'And am I supposed to be flattered by that?' she demanded tartly.

Running his hand through his hair, Drake said, 'I had to tell you how I felt. I'm not asking you to do anything about it, but I can't go on pretending that I don't care about you.' His voice was harsh with tension.

Her heart skipped a beat, filled with shattering expectation and hope. She waited for him to go on but he didn't and she said gropingly, 'So—so this isn't a proposition, then?'

'No. Not, that is, unless...'

She realised then that he was leaving it entirely to her, that his idea of caring was entirely different from hers, and a spurt of humiliated fury fired her temper. 'Not unless I say, Sure, fine, your place or mine? Is that it?'

'Something like that,' Drake admitted.

'How dare you? How dare you think that you only have to say you want me and I'll fall into bed with you?'

'I thought that you weren't—uninterested.'

Ignoring that, Allie said angrily, 'And is this how you usually proposition the women you want? By being cold and aloof, then leaving them to make the running, to do the asking? Just what kind of a man are you?'

Rounding on her, Drake suddenly took hold of her arms. 'The kind who can't sleep at night from thinking about you, the kind who can't wait for the time to meet you again, who longs to see you. The kind of man who has an ache inside him that's as real and fierce as a physical pain. I want you more than I've wanted a woman for a very long time.'

His vehemence astounded her; from being cool and withdrawn he'd suddenly become a man of fierce passions. But she was still annoyed and said, '*You* want. It's always *you*. And just where do I figure in all this?'

'Can you deny that you feel the same way?'

'Sure I can,' she said at once, still angry. 'If you must know I'm *completely* indifferent to you. I wouldn't want you if you were the only man left after Armageddon. I wouldn't want you if every other man on earth dissolved into dust. I wouldn't—'

But Drake had had enough. Pulling her to him, he said roughly, 'Allie, for heaven's sake shut up and come here.' And, putting his arms firmly round her, he kissed her.

She was swamped by his need of her. Any resistance just got lost beneath the onslaught of his lips. The hunger in him was a tangible thing, a fierce greed for fulfilment, a flame that wanted to devour her. His body trembled with the uncontrollable strength of his desire, and he groaned against her mouth, his breath ragged and gasping. Allie had never known such violent passion before. This was no kiss that would lead to a civilised seduction, this was a full-blooded, desperate cry of frustration which completely overwhelmed her. He drank of her mouth like a man close to dying of thirst, and his hot lips seared her neck, her throat in frantic kisses before returning with fierce insistence to her mouth.

Then Drake's hands went down to her hips, held her close against him as he moved, exciting himself beyond endurance, until he flung back his head in a cry of frustration that was more an agonising groan of pain. 'Allie. Oh, God, Allie.' Lifting an unsteady hand, he cupped her face and looked down at her.

His touch was very hot and there was the perspiration of extreme emotion on his skin. Allie's hands were against his chest and she could feel the tremors of awareness that ran through him, the unsteady beat of his heart. His need for her excited her, turned her on. She covered his hand with her own, turned her head so that she could kiss his palm, then his fingers, let her tongue as well as her lips caress him.

He cried out, the fingers of his other hand, the one that held her so close, digging into her, bruising her skin. He gasped, groaned out her name again on a note of supplication, but then couldn't stand it any more and snatched his hand away. Allie was wearing a dress with thin shoulder straps and he pulled them down without finesse, too hungry for anything but the immediate satisfaction of desire. Her skin gleamed, pale as silk, soft as velvet in the moonlight, her nipples small, delicious buds that drove him crazy with delight as he lifted shaking hands to touch, caress.

'God, you're beautiful, so beautiful. A porcelain doll.'

But he wasn't treating her like a doll. His fingers wrought delight, awakening her nerve-ends, filling her with the most erotic desire as he toyed with her. Then he bent to kiss her there and she gave a low moan of primitive pleasure. Her body arched under him, wanted him to go on, to never stop.

Drake lifted his head, his breath hot, uneven, his hands shaking with need. He saw her eyes closed as she lived within the bodily delight he'd awakened in her, saw her mouth parted in desire. 'Now can you say you're not interested?' he demanded, his voice thick and urgent.

'No,' she breathed. 'No, I can't deny it.' Allie lifted heavy lids, her eyes dark with her own need.

He gave a long, shuddering sigh of satisfaction. Sure of her now, Drake caressed her more gently, then gave each small, upstanding nipple a long kiss before drawing the straps of her dress back onto her shoulders. Taking her hand, he went to lead her back to the car, but she stood still. 'I'm taking you back to my flat,' he explained.

Slowly she shook her head.

His hand clenched hers. 'I thought it was what you wanted.' His voice was harsh, wary.

'It is. But—I'm sorry. It isn't convenient. We'll have to wait a few days.'

His shoulders sagged and Drake put his hands up to cover his face for a moment, then gave a short, mirthless laugh. But then he said, 'So it's just the timing that's wrong?'

'Yes.' Putting her hands on his shoulders, Allie stretched on tiptoe to kiss him on the mouth. It was a very slow, sensuous kiss, her lips exploring, her tongue darting to touch his, but refusing to be drawn into passion. It was a kiss of promise, a hint of her deep sexuality. When his hands tightened and his breath became a ragged moan of frustration, she took her mouth from his at last and said on a low, seductive note, 'But think how much more exciting it will be when we finally get together.'

'You're a witch,' Drake murmured unsteadily. He kissed her throat. 'An enchantress.' He went on kissing her for a while, reluctant to let her go, wanting to prolong this but at the same time knowing that it would only make his frustration deeper.

It was Allie who finally drew back and, taking his hand, led him to the car.

Back at her hotel he parked outside and kissed her again with deep hunger, long and lingeringly. Allie laughed at him gently. 'Hey, we can't stay here all night, you know.'

'I don't want to let you go. The longer I keep you with me, the sooner the time will pass.'

She caressed his face. 'We'll go to bed,' she assured him, touching her lips to his. 'That's a promise.'

Then she slipped out of the car and walked across the pavement to the hotel. For the first time Drake didn't come with her, but contented himself with watching to make sure she got there safely.

In bed that night Allie felt a glow of warm excitement, was brimful of happiness. OK, he hadn't said he loved her, but Drake's lovemaking had been fiery, exhilarating, had aroused a need that was far deeper than anything she had experienced for a long time, perhaps ever. She felt that she could well be on the verge of what promised to be a very fulfilling relationship at the least, and at the most...? Who knew? It could perhaps lead to something far more lasting.

And Allie found, almost to her own surprise, that she wanted that very desperately. That she should even consider it was a novelty; she'd been so busy shaping her career that the prospect of a permanent relationship had always been something for the remote future. But she liked Drake as well as loved him, could imagine him being the kind of partner who was a friend, an intelligent companion, as well as a lover. He had been cool at times, admittedly, but tonight had more than made up for that. And if he lacked ambition that could perhaps be changed. Yes, a relationship with Drake promised great potential. Allie found herself full of hope for the future, which, where a man was concerned, was a whole new and wonderful experience for her. And besides—she smiled in the darkness—when he'd kissed her the world had started to spin and her insides had definitely done a somersault. And she couldn't wait to sample more of the same.

The euphoric feeling was still there when she woke the next day and Allie lay savouring it for a while. Her thoughts were full of tender feelings about Drake; she could imagine how wonderful the next few days would be as they got to really know each other, close but not yet intimate. And how even more fantastic it would be when they finally went to bed together. Life was suddenly really great, with the expectation of being even brighter, perhaps for ever.

The phone rang while she was in the shower and she had to run, naked but for a small towel, to answer it. It was Bob, her boss.

'How are things going?'

'Oh, fine.'

'How much longer do you think the job will take?'

'Possibly another two weeks,' Allie told him, her fingers crossed as she told the white lie. With the research help that Drake had given her it wouldn't take that long, but she needed a few days for her own purposes.

But Bob seemed perfectly happy with that and said, 'How are you getting on with Drake?'

She smiled at her reflection in the mirror over the dressing-table but kept her voice nonchalant as she said, 'Oh, OK, I suppose.'

'He's still in Moscow, then?'

'Yes, I think so.'

'I saw his parents a couple of days ago,' Bob explained. 'They said he was due back in England but hadn't arrived. They'd just been to visit his fiancée.'

The world suddenly seemed to stand still, and the morning became just another day. 'His fiancée?' Allie repeated hollowly.

'Yes, he— Oh, darn. Look, Allie, I'll have to go; I've got a signal that another caller is waiting and I know it's important. Phone me a couple of days before you're ready to leave or if you have any problems. Bye.'

Slowly she replaced the receiver, the happiness gone and anger filling her heart.

For their answer Harry spilt the milk and said 'How about getting on with bricks?'

She stared at her reflection in the mirror over the dresser took out kept her voice confident to the wall, The UK rates from London to the ...... a mile of Moscow .....

CHAPTER FOUR

HALF an hour later the phone rang again. This time it was Drake.

'Good morning.' His voice was warm, with a touch of possessiveness. 'I hope you slept well.'

'Like a log. Did you?' Allie tried to betray nothing in her voice although it nearly choked her even to speak to him.

'I didn't want to. I wanted to think about you all night.'

'But you fell asleep,' she guessed. 'And I bet you didn't even dream about me.'

Drake laughed. 'If I could have commanded my dreams they would have been full of you.'

'And no one else?' she asked lightly.

'Definitely of no one else.'

Allie gritted her teeth. The hypocrite. The louse!

'I'll meet you this afternoon. At the hotel,' Drake said, confident she was his to order around.

'No, I might be late today. Look, you're always taking me out; why don't I take you out tonight instead?' Allie suggested.

'That really isn't necessary. And what does it matter so long as I'm with you?'

Her hand tightened on the receiver but she said, 'No, I insist. Give me your address and I'll pick *you* up. Around eight.'

'I'd feel a lot happier if we went in my car.'

'But then it wouldn't be my treat,' Allie protested. 'Please, let me do this my way, Drake. It will be fun.'

He laughed, and said reluctantly, 'All right. But be careful, won't you? Take a registered taxi and make sure the doorman shows him the address and he knows where to go.'

Her smile was cold but her voice flirtatious as Allie said, 'Why, Drake, anyone would think you cared.'

But his tone was one of deep sincerity as he replied, 'I do. You know that. And I can't wait to show you how much.'

Today they were photographing the Clover Egg, the one that had lost its surprise. She had deliberately left this one till the last although it was a day she had been greatly but secretly looking forward to. But now she would rather it had been any other day than this. It was so difficult to concentrate when she was still seething about Drake. She wondered if it had all been an act, his coolness deliberately assumed to arouse her interest. And his passion and apparently desperate need for her last night; had that, too, all been a pretence? Was it just an unusual, but admittedly very successful, line?

Allie had to drag her thoughts back to her work. The museum staff had become so used to her now that usually there were only two people with her: an assistant who would move the egg around and place it on the turntable, and a guard who sat by the door out of the way. One or the other of these would quite often go outside and not come back for some time. It was during one of these periods, when the assistant had left her to her photography and the guard was lounging in his chair, half asleep in a room hot not only from the sun outside but also from the strong artificial lighting, his uniform cap shading his eyes, that Allie made a full-scale drawing of the egg. And onto this she couldn't resist sketching the details she'd been given, so long ago, of the missing surprise. Hearing footsteps returning, she quickly stowed the sketch in her bag and was busy behind the camera when the assistant came back in and the guard straightened up.

Sergei came at lunchtime and again invited her out, but half-heartedly, sure that she was going to turn him down. But Allie smiled at him and said, 'I'm really grateful for all you've done to help me, so why don't I take you out tonight?'

He didn't need much persuading and even provided a few suggestions for places where they could eat.

So it was that when the taxi pulled up outside his building that evening Drake, who was waiting at the entrance, went to get into the back of the cab and found Sergei already sitting next to Allie, on her other side. He had been all ready to greet her warmly, take her in his arms and kiss her, but was brought up short by the presence of the other man.

Allie moved up obligingly, saying, 'Yes, come in the back. There's plenty of room.'

The movement had brought her close to Sergei and he put an arm across the back of the seat, almost resting on her shoulder.

There was restrained surprise and puzzlement in

Drake's voice as he joined them and said, 'Hello, Sergei. Nice to see you.'

The surprise was echoed in Sergei's voice as he returned the greeting and it was evident to Allie that neither man was pleased to see the other but both were too polite to let it show.

They chatted easily enough on the way to the restaurant and when they got there Allie took care to again sit between the two of them. The restaurant was in a luxurious eighteenth-century mansion and, after looking round, Allie smiled at them and said, 'Isn't this wonderful?'

Sergei grinned and nodded; he at least was enjoying the evening for the food and the ambience if for nothing else. If he felt any chagrin at not being alone with her he contrived to hide it, instead chatting expansively, and even more so by the time they got to the second bottle of wine. Drake, too, was amicable and polite but at the first opportunity asked her to dance.

'Why did you invite him along?' he demanded, almost as soon as he had taken her in his arms.

'Do you mind?'

'I wanted to be alone with you.' Drake's voice was soft, his eyes tender.

'I owed him a meal. Would you rather I'd gone out alone with him?'

'No.' Drake's arm tightened and he smiled down at her. 'It's just that I spent the whole day looking forward to being with you.'

'Really?'

His face sharpened with need and his tone grew urgent. 'I want desperately to kiss you, Allie.'

There was such yearning in his eyes, his voice that Allie's heart lurched even though she knew this was all just a charade. 'Hey,' she chided. 'You mustn't say things like that. You'll make me blush.'

'I would *love* to make you blush.'

She lifted her head and looked into his eyes, trying to pierce through his veneer of duplicity. But there was only warmth and tenderness in his face, a slight curl of a smile on his lips, and undisguised attraction in his gaze. He looked like the man he had pretended to be last night: an eager lover, a man who couldn't wait to make her his. Allie looked away. A slight flush of colour did come into her cheeks, making Drake smile, but it was of anger and mortification rather than the embarrassment he imagined.

He went to draw her closer but she moved away, and said tightly, 'We'd better get back to Sergei.'

'No, I want to go on holding you.'

When Drake did things he didn't do them by halves, Allie thought. From being cool and aloof he had changed completely, become instead a man of fire who wasn't afraid to hide it. If she hadn't known better she would have believed him to have been almost afraid to admit his feelings about her earlier, but, having decided she was what he wanted, then he had determined to hold nothing back, to give full rein to his passion for her. Only she did know better, and his hypocrisy sickened her. But two could play at that game. So she smiled and said softly, 'And I want you to hold me. But is that fair on either of us when we have to wait?'

Drake groaned a little and she knew that he wanted

to hold her really close, to feel her body against the length of his. But she had judged him accurately, and he drew away, too civilised to do so in a public place, and especially with Sergei looking on.

Going back to the table, she ordered a bottle of champagne, but no amount of the rich wine could take away the nasty taste in her mouth that Drake's duplicity had caused.

Later she danced with the Russian. 'Shall I hold you very close and make Drake jealous?' he asked her with a grin.

She gave him a slightly startled look and then smiled back. 'What makes you think he'd be jealous?'

Sergei gave a theatrical shudder. 'Already I can feel his eyes like daggers in my back. He would like me to turn to dust so that he can have you all to himself.'

'I'm sure you're wrong,' Allie protested.

'But isn't that why I'm here—to make him jealous?'

'Certainly not.'

Sergei looked more interested. 'Am I the one who is supposed to get jealous, then?'

Allie raised her eyebrows in amused exasperation. 'Men! This is purely my way of saying thank you to *both* of you for the help you've given me here. Personalities don't come into it.'

'That is impossible,' Sergei corrected her firmly. 'Where a beautiful woman like you is concerned there will always be personal feelings—jealousy, love.'

He said it suggestively, his eyes attempting to hold hers, but Allie merely gave an amused shake of her head and looked away, then began to chat about

Moscow, hoping to divert him. Glancing across the room at Drake, she saw that he was watching them, but there was no jealousy in his face, rather a sort of tolerant amusement, almost as if she were a toy he had allowed someone else to play with for a while but would soon take back. The china doll that he had called her, perhaps. Seeing her looking at him, Drake smiled, one full of meaning. It was a mixture of a shared secret, of impatience, but also of utter confidence that they would soon become lovers. Yesterday Allie would have enjoyed such a message, would have returned it, but not now. Definitely not now.

Inwardly irrationally angry, Allie walked back to their table with Sergei and found it hard to return Drake's smile as he politely stood up, his manners exquisite as always. When your feelings threatened to overwhelm you and you couldn't hide them, then there was only one thing a woman could do. Allie did it; she excused herself and picked up her bag to go to the ladies'-room. But as she turned she bumped into a large man from the next table who was just returning to his seat. The bag fell from her hand, bursting open as it hit the floor and the contents spilling out. Immediately both Drake and Sergei bent to pick up the scattered make-up stuff, pens, money, cards—all the things that her bag was always stuffed with. It was Sergei who picked up the drawing that she'd done earlier that day. He glanced at it idly, then more closely.

Allie felt her skin tighten and she quickly crouched down and began to take the things from them. 'How clumsy of me. I know I shouldn't carry so much around but you never know when you're going to need them. Thanks.' She took a handful of things from Drake, reached for the sketch in Sergei's hand.

He was frowning at it. 'What is this, Allie?'

'That?' She took it from him, glanced at it casually. 'Oh, that's just a lighting sketch I did for today's egg. I do one every day before I shoot each egg.' She tried to keep her voice light but was aware that Drake was watching her. He put a hand over hers for a second and she looked down, saw that her knuckles had gone white. Forcing herself to relax, she stood up and glanced round. 'I think that's everything. Thanks. Excuse me.' And she hurried out of the dining-room.

Damn! Allie stood in the Ladies and cursed, wondering just how familiar Sergei was with the Fabergé eggs. She thought she'd managed to cover up quite well, but she knew he only had to go and look at the collection to know that the surprise was missing from the Clover Egg. But would he say anything? Would he report this? It was only a small thing after all. Not that his reaction mattered too much, because Allie knew that if she had managed to deceive Sergei she had certainly not deceived Drake. He had sensed and then seen the tension in her. He would want an explanation, and he would demand it as soon as they were alone.

So she had better make sure they weren't alone until she could get away from Moscow, and forget about him for ever.

Lip-sticking a bright smile on her face, Allie went back to the dining-room. The two of them were talking but in a casual way; their heads weren't close

together as they would be if they were talking about
the drawing, about her. But the eyes of both men studied her as she walked up to them. Drake asked her to
dance again but Allie declined and sat down, began
to ask about the building they were in, who had
owned it, keeping them both talking until it was, at
last, time to leave.

Last to be picked up, Drake was the first to be
dropped off, although he didn't like it. In fact he invited them both up to his flat for a nightcap, but Allie,
touching his hand lightly, said that she was rather
tired.

'Of course. But give me a moment, will you?' And,
getting out of the cab, he drew her after him. Taking
her hand, he carried it to his mouth, turning it over
so that his lips, hard and sensuous, caressed her palm.
She shivered and sighed at the frisson of desire it sent
running through her. 'Tomorrow?' Drake said softly,
still holding her hand.

Unable to speak, she nodded, her lips parted in
awareness.

His hand tightened on hers but then he let her go
and said in a normal tone, 'Thanks for a marvellous
evening.' He helped her back into the cab, said goodnight to Sergei, and waved as he watched it pull away.

Sergei chuckled as Allie casually moved along the
seat away from him. 'I will make a bet with you.'

'Oh? What's that?'

'I bet that Drake will be on the phone to your room
two minutes after you arrive there.'

She smiled but said, 'Why should he do that?'

'To make sure that I haven't kidnapped you.'

'That's hardly likely.'

'No.' Sergei spoke regretfully. 'But if this had been a hundred years ago, then I would definitely have abducted you and taken you to my dacha.'

'Your dacha?' Allie pretended ignorance. 'What's that?'

'Dachas are the small houses in the country that all the city people go to in the summer. Those that can afford them and have a car to get there.'

'Do you have one?'

'My parents do. They go there for the whole of the summer.'

'Don't you go?'

'Occasionally, but the city is more fun.' They fell silent for a moment, then Sergei said, 'Tell me, Allie, how much longer will you be here in Moscow?'

'I'm not absolutely certain,' she replied easily. 'All the films I've taken have been sent to London to be processed; if my boss is unhappy with anything I've done then it will have to be photographed again. And then I have some more research to do on the background of the Fabergé factory.' She smiled at him. 'Perhaps you could spare some time to help me with that? For a payment to cover your time, of course.'

He seemed pleased by the idea and they discussed it until she dropped him off at his apartment block. She hadn't told him that Drake had already done most of the research for her; but anyway it always paid to have the work double-checked. And she hadn't told him that he would be left to do the work on his own, but so long as she paid him she didn't think that Sergei would mind too much. She would mail him a list of the research to be done, along with a note explaining that she had had to leave Moscow quite suddenly. A duplicate of the note she would leave at the hotel for Drake.

Once back at the hotel, as she went to the desk to ask for her key, Allie remembered Sergei's bet that Drake would phone, so she told the receptionist that she didn't want to be disturbed. Which should take care of that problem.

She stayed up late that night, writing out the list and the note for Sergei, putting them into an envelope together with the money to cover the work, then writing out the note for Drake. Allie found the latter really hard to do. The trouble was that she wanted to leave him sweet, thinking that she really regretted having to leave Russia, to leave him, while all the while she felt angry at the way he'd lied, the way he'd tried to fool her. Hating herself for the hypocrisy *she* was forced to use, Allie told him how disappointed she was to have to leave—'for family reasons', as she put it—and finished by saying she hoped they would be able to get together in London. Which should be safe enough, she decided; Drake was hardly likely to risk having an affair right under the nose of his fiancée.

The phone rang the next morning but she ignored it and skipped breakfast as she packed all her things, carefully taking the little book and the road map from the safe and putting them in her bag. Her intention was to leave the hotel at the usual time and walk round to the Kremlin, taking with her a shopping bag laden with gifts for the museum staff. But everyone was going out at this time of the day and the lifts, as always, were busy. Having waited a few minutes, Allie became impatient and went down by the stairs instead. At the mezzanine she automatically glanced over the balcony and then hastily drew back. Drake was there. He was sitting in a chair and glancing half-heartedly at a paper as he waited for her to come down.

For a moment she panicked, but then remembered that there must be a service staircase somewhere in the building. She found it and went hastily down, finding herself in a corridor leading to the kitchens. But at the far end she glimpsed daylight and eventually came out at the back of the hotel and was able to lose herself in the commuter crowds on the nearest street.

Having hurried, Allie arrived at the entrance to the museum only a few minutes later than usual. The guards at the gate knew her by now and returned her greeting of '*Dobraya utra*' with grins of welcome. Inside the museum she said goodbye to the professor and his staff and gave them the presents she'd brought with her: champagne and caviare for the professor, wine and chocolates for his assistants, and vodka for the guard. They helped her pack her equipment and she gave Professor Martos one of her cameras that he'd openly admired and coveted. Overwhelming her with thanks, the professor got out his car and drove Allie back to the hotel.

When they got there she touched the professor's arm and said confidingly, 'Please could you be very kind and do something for me? There's a man, an Englishman, who's being a pain.' Professor Martos frowned in puzzlement, and she explained, 'He's being a nuisance. He won't leave me alone. Could you, please, look to make sure he isn't waiting in the hotel?' And she described Drake to him.

The professor, his chivalry appealed to, assured her that she had nothing to fear with him around and obligingly went to look. He was back a few minutes later and told her there was no sign of a man of Drake's description. Relieved, Allie said goodbye to him and hurried inside.

Within twenty minutes Allie had checked out and was in a taxi on her way to the airport, the letter for Sergei and the note for Drake left with the receptionist to pass on. But she was still tense, still afraid that somehow Drake might still be looking for her, might have seen her get into the taxi and be following. So at the airport Allie was very careful, standing still and looking all around before she made a move, and only when she was absolutely certain that Drake was nowhere to be seen did she at last make her way to a desk. But she didn't check in for a flight, instead hiring a car for the next week. A small Russian-made car that was exactly like thousands of others that thronged the streets and were frequently to be seen broken down at the side of the road. Praying that this one would be more reliable, she packed her things into the boot, took out the map book she had bought on her first day in Moscow and headed east out of the city. She was soon caught up in the traffic, took a few turns to make sure she was lost among it, and only when she was again sure that she'd not been followed did she turn onto the road that took her north and would eventually finish up at St Petersburg.

Once on it she smiled with relief and mounting excited anticipation. The sun was shining and the road was good. She was at last setting out on the hunt that would be the biggest adventure of her life—and keeping the promise to her great-grandmother who had lived and danced in Russia so many years ago. Before the revolution, before she had had to flee for her life, leaving her treasure behind.

CHAPTER FIVE

IT WAS a long way from Moscow to St Petersburg and most people either flew or took a sleeper train, but Allie wanted to appear to be a tourist so didn't hurry, and to that end took a side road to look at a monastery when she saw the silver onion domes on the skyline. She spent the night at a small hotel in a town only a hundred miles from Moscow, speaking Russian to the staff. Here she filled the car with petrol and set off again early the next morning.

Another beautiful day; Allie drove into another town where she stopped for lunch and bought a garden spade from the local market. This she stowed under her suitcase in the boot before she drove on. The roads weren't so good now; potholes that had appeared in the winter hadn't been filled in and had been made deeper by lorries, so she had to go more slowly to avoid them. Two hours later she stopped to look at her road map and then turned onto a side road, her eyes scanning the skyline.

Twenty miles on she saw what she was looking for, an old mill poised on the distant skyline. There didn't seem to be a direct road to it so Allie was forced to stop at a garage where she bought a drink and asked for directions to reach it. Following the garage attendant's pointing arm, she turned into a bumpy, overgrown lane and crawled along until she stopped in the shadow of some trees near the mill. The ancient building was entirely made of wood and was still working, its double sails groaning round in the breeze, its timbers shaded to silver by long years of weathering.

Allie watched it for a while, feeling timeless, then looked around her. There were several small wooden houses dotted around the fields, the dachas that Sergei had described to her. A young woman with a child in her arms came out of one and walked over to her, saying a tentative hello. She looked surprised when Allie returned the greeting in her own language but was soon telling her about the mill, about the child, about herself.

Most of what the woman said Allie could understand or guess at, and she found that she was enjoying herself. The countryside was so beautiful, so peaceful, and it was fun to practise her Russian. On impulse Allie gave a sweep of her arm and said, 'These dachas; is there one I could rent? An empty one where I could stay for a day or two?'

The woman, who had introduced herself as Ludmilla, nodded at once. 'Yes, there is one that I look after for the owners. But they do not come this summer. Would you like to see it?'

They got in the car and drove down an earth track, sending up a cloud of dust from the wheels, for about half a mile, skirting a lake that had a small island in its centre. The dacha they eventually came to was again of weather-beaten wood, had only one storey but had ornate architraves over the door and windows, speaking of an attempt by the original owners to give a touch of grandeur to the place. Inside it was immaculately clean if rather bare. There was the usual large stove on one wall of the main L-shaped room and a table with benches on two sides at the corner near the window.

In the corner there was also a simple icon on the wall and under it a white cloth, like a linen towel, embroidered in bright red colours. A couple of modern armchairs that had seen much better days stood on either side of the stove, and in the same room, but in the space that formed a right angle to the rest was a simple double bed built into an alcove in the wall, and a cupboard and chest for clothes. The rest of the building was given over to a large storeroom containing an old sled, and piles of wood for the stove, essential for anyone who lived here in the wintertime, and a primitive bathroom with a footbath and a chemical loo.

Apart from a couple of outbuildings, that was it. There was no electricity, of course, but there was Calor gas and water could be had from a pump at the end of the lane. Allie was enchanted with it and immediately agreed a price, paying Ludmilla in advance and also buying enough groceries from her to last for a couple of days; just simple stuff: eggs, cheese, bread and milk, coffee.

'You will eat with us tonight,' the latter insisted, and went away happy when Allie agreed.

It was a simple meal of borscht—a soup red from the beetroot it contained which was almost a meal in itself—followed by blinys—pancakes served with soured cream. Ludmilla's husband was away, working in the town and only coming home for the weekends.

Obviously lonely, she kept Allie talking as long as she could, but the mental concentration this took was enervating, so Allie pleaded tiredness from driving, which was true enough, and thanked her hostess for the meal. Ludmilla couldn't leave the baby so Allie walked back to the dacha alone, not minding in the least as she paced along the rutted track beneath a sky of velvet studded with stars, the way made almost as light as day by the brilliance of the full moon.

But the moon cast long shadows from the trees she passed and the side of the dacha where the door was situated was also in the blackness of deep shadow. Allie groped for the key above the lintel, unlocked the door and pushed it open. She stepped inside and went to shut the door but it was suddenly flung out of her hand as a man leaped out of the darkness outside and spun her round, pushing her into the house! Allie started to give an instinctive scream but she was grabbed from behind and a hand was put over her mouth. Her heart filled with terror and she had the immediate female dread of rape. But then a man's voice—Drake's voice—said in her ear, 'You know, Allie, I rather think you've got lost. This road definitely doesn't lead to the airport.'

Slowly she relaxed, her body sagging as the abject terror left her. Drake took his hand away and let her stand. Not afraid now that she knew it was him but still shaking, she said unsteadily, 'God, you frightened me half to death.'

'Did I?'

His tone, cold and withdrawn, suddenly brought her back to her senses and Allie drew in her breath sharply. What was he *doing* here? *How on earth had he found her?* Slowly she turned to face him, her mind panicking, brain racing. Why wasn't he safely left behind in Moscow, reading the letter that was supposed to put him off the scent? And, oh, Lord, how was she going to handle this?

It was too dark to see him clearly, all she could see was the outline of his figure in the moonlight that shone through the uncurtained window on the other side of the room. Her voice tense, she said, 'I can't see you. I'll light the lamp.'

'No, I'll do it.' Without fumbling or searching around, Drake strode to the table and lit the oil lamp that stood on it. The mellow golden light slowly heightened, filling the room until only the far corners were in shadow. Drake replaced the glass shade and then lifted his head to look at her.

His features were very sharp, tense, his mouth drawn into a thin line, his eyes cold. 'I think you have some explaining to do,' he said tersely.

Allie looked at him for a moment, then said, 'You've been in here before. You know your way around.'

He nodded. 'That's right; I found the key and came in earlier, but decided to wait outside to see where you came from.'

'Why?'

Drake gave a laugh that wasn't at all pleasant. 'My dear Allie, we had a date, if you remember. I don't like being stood up. It isn't good for my image.'

She stared in astonishment. 'You came after me because of *that*?'

'Oh, no—not only that.'

His voice was silky, menacing, and she remembered with sickening clarity the way he'd guessed
there was something wrong when Sergei had looked
at her sketch of the Clover Egg. Well, his thoughts
must be distracted from that—at all costs. Kicking off
her shoes, Allie went to sit near the table, her legs
curled under her on the bench, her back against the
wall.

'So how did you find me?'

Coming across, Drake sat on the bench opposite her
and leaned his elbows on the table, interlocking his
fingers as he said, 'It wasn't difficult. I rang Bob to
find out why you'd been called home but he, of
course, knew nothing about it. He was afraid that
something might have happened to one of your family
so he contacted them and—lo and behold—they
didn't know anything either. So it became something
of a mystery.' He paused reflectively. 'I rather enjoy
mysteries, and this one had become, shall we say,
rather personal.' His facial expression hadn't changed
but the last two words had a menacing emphasis.

'Luckily I know an official who works at the airport,' he went on. 'I got him to find out which flight
you'd caught, but wasn't altogether surprised when he
reported that you hadn't booked on any flight leaving
the country. It didn't take him long to find out that
you'd hired a car instead.'

'Very clever,' Allie observed. 'But I could have left
Moscow in any direction.'

Drake nodded. 'It became more difficult, admittedly, but you forget that this country was closed to

foreigners for many years; they're still a novelty away from the main cities. I worked out how far you could go on a tank of petrol and rang all the garages around that radius from Moscow to ask for a blonde English woman driving alone. It took quite a while and I admit I almost didn't find you, because the garage where you had stopped said that they'd seen a woman who answered the description I gave, but she had spoken Russian.' He gave a small laugh. 'It was only when I'd drawn a blank at the other petrol stations I tried that I put two and two together—and came up with a very interesting conclusion.'

Allie shrugged, said lightly, 'I always try to learn some of the language of every country I go to. I always think it's rather arrogant to expect everyone to speak English.'

'And you learnt it well enough to make the garage owner think you were a native. You must have a very good ear,' he said with heavy sarcasm.

But Allie retorted, 'Yes, I have. I was always good at languages. That's one of the reasons why Bob sends me abroad on these assignments.'

'Oh, yes, Bob. You told him that you had another two weeks' work to do.'

'I was tired. I needed a holiday,' Allie said defensively. 'And I wanted to see something of the country so I decided to drive to St Petersburg.'

'Surely Bob would have given you the holiday if you'd asked him?'

Allie's mouth drew into a petulant *moue*. 'You don't know him as an employer. He wants to get this CD-ROM finished so that he can market it. He expected me to go straight from here to the States and keep on with the work.'

'You make him out to be a slave-driver,' Drake remarked. 'I hardly recognise him from your description.'

'Like I said, you don't work for him.'

Leaning forward, Drake leaned his chin on his hands. 'Now, I wonder why I don't believe you?'

She shrugged. 'It doesn't matter whether you believe me or not. What matters is why you're here. Why you followed me.'

Drake's eyebrows rose at the distinct challenge. 'I think you know why.'

Her blue eyes met his unflinchingly. 'Yes, I suppose I do. You want sex.'

His breath drew in with a hiss at her directness. 'That's a very crude way of putting it.'

'Isn't it true?'

He paused for a moment, his face set, then said, 'Yes.'

It was as if someone had just wired the room, made it hot with electric tension. Drake's face was taut, the skin tight across rigid cheekbones, but it was his eyes that gave him away. Even shadowed by the lamplight they were dark with need, with sexual arousal.

Getting to her feet, Allie went over to the Calor gas ring and found the matches to light it. 'You must think me a terrible hostess,' she remarked. 'Would you like a drink? There's coffee, or a cola if you would prefer it.' She gave a small shrug. 'Nothing very exciting, I'm afraid—but then I didn't know that you were going to turn up, did I?'

Her tone was sardonic, making Drake say abruptly, 'Why did you run away?'

'"Run away"!' She gave a mocking laugh. 'How melodramatic you make it sound. Do you want coffee or not?'

'No!' Drake was suddenly beside her and had spun her round. 'Stop playing games. I want the truth.'

She glared up at him. 'Let go of my arm.'

For a long moment their eyes were locked in challenging combat, then Drake slowly let her go. 'Why?' he demanded.

'Just what right do you have to ask me questions?' she said angrily. 'I shall do as I darn well please.'

'You seem to forget that we had an understanding.'

'Oh, that.' She shrugged it off. 'I had no intention of going to bed with you.'

His face tightened. 'So why agree to it?'

'You were so eager; I didn't want to deflate your ego by telling you that I wasn't interested.' She gave him an ironical look from under her lashes. 'One tries to be kind to the male sex, you know. Leave them with their macho image of themselves still intact.'

Drake crossed his arms, his fingers pressing into his own skin. Dryly, he said, 'You didn't behave as if you weren't interested. Quite the opposite, in fact.'

'Again, an act. I didn't want you for an enemy, after all.' She paused to lend emphasis to her next words. 'But I sure as hell didn't want you for a lover. I have rather high standards where that's concerned.'

His cheeks flinched at the insult, but then Drake shook his head. 'Oh, no, I don't buy that. You were as hot for it as I was.'

'Really? Then why did I lie and say I wasn't available?'

'Was it a lie?'

'I've just said so.' But she had been telling the truth and only now chose to deceive him.

His face cold as stone, Drake stared at her for a moment, then abruptly turned and went back to his seat.

He was silent as she made the coffee in two cracked mugs and took them over to the table, and only then did he say heavily, 'So why did you lie?'

Allie took a moment to sip her coffee. It was necessary to make him think her hard, heartless and unfeeling, when she wasn't like that at all. She didn't want to, it went against her nature to be cruel to anyone. But hadn't he been cruel to her? Hadn't he set out to make her fall for him, to seduce her? When all the time he was engaged to some other girl. So what did that make him? In Allie's book an engagement ring was as binding as a wedding ring, and she had no time for men who thought they could still play around until the knot was actually tied. They were the sort of men who took promises and vows too lightly, who would be unfaithful at the first opportunity that came along. And she was darned if she was going to be Drake's opportunity. She had wanted to be rid of him from the start but now the motive was truly personal.

So, her voice coolly mocking and slightly impatient, she said, 'Oh, come on; surely you recognise a put-down when you hear it? It's all part of the game, Drake. Or, if you prefer it, the war between the sexes.

We had a skirmish, a minor flirtation to see what might come of it. But I wasn't turned on and I certainly didn't want to go any further. So I lied.' She lifted an arm in a throw-away gesture. 'It's a lie all women use as an excuse when they want out of a situation. Surely you know that?'

'Not the women I know,' he rejoined tightly.

'Well, lucky you. Or is it that you haven't much experience of women?'

'Of your type of woman, evidently not.'

Allie's hand tightened on her mug and she would have liked to throw it at him. Damn him! He was the one who was a louse. He had charmed her, intrigued her, until she had fallen in love with him. And she had *wanted* to go to bed with him, had trusted him enough to agree to give herself to him. It was a long time since that had happened to her and it would, she realised, now be even longer before she trusted another man as much.

She gave a derisory laugh. 'So now we've both insulted each other why don't you finish your drink and get the hell out?'

He shook his head. 'Oh, no, you don't get rid of me that easily. You're playing games but they're not sex games. You want me out of the way so that you can do whatever it is that you came here for.'

Allie gave an impatient gesture. 'I've finished my work for Bob. And I deserve a holiday.'

With a mock-curious look, Drake said, 'Tell me, do you ever tell the truth about anything, Allie?'

Refusing to be intimidated, she said drawlingly, 'You really don't know much about women, do you?'

'I suppose by that you mean a woman will always lie when it suits her. There are some women who would never stoop to it,' he told her with a definite sneer in his voice.

'Maybe it's just that you haven't caught them out,' Allie responded with false sweetness. Her voice hardened. 'I don't want you here, Drake. Just leave, will you?'

'No. I have nowhere to go so here is as good as any other place. And please don't go to the bother of thinking up some way to make me leave because I intend to stay here until you tell me what it is you're up to.'

'I'm not—' she began.

But Drake cut in, 'With regard to the Clover Egg.'

So there it was, out in the open. Allie's face tightened, but she managed to give a surprised laugh. 'What? What are you talking about?'

'You already know, so don't pretend ignorance. You had a sketch of the egg in your bag at the restaurant the other night. Complete with a drawing of the novelty that went inside it. Only—surprise, surprise—when I went to the museum yesterday to check I found that the novelty has been lost and there is only a written description of what the egg should have contained.'

'I know,' Allie said calmly. 'I read the description and did the drawing based on it. For the CD-ROM. To let the buyers know what it would have looked like. When I get back to England I'll get one of the artists at the company to do a professional painting of it so that we can superimpose the drawing on the egg. So what's so wonderful about that?'

Putting his hands together, Drake gave her a slow round of applause. 'Very good,' he said admiringly. 'I could almost have believed you. But then, you've given me every reason to know what a good and habitual liar you are.' He suddenly leaned forward, taking her by surprise and making her flinch back. 'But you forget that I saw the panic in your eyes, felt it in your hands when Sergei picked up that drawing. You're playing some deep game, Allie, and I want to know what it is.'

He was on such dangerous ground. She had to lead him away, even if it was onto ground that was as treacherous as quicksand. '*I'm* playing games?' She laughed. 'Oh, no, you're the one who's doing that. *And* you're the one who's lying through their teeth. Do you really expect me to believe you came after me because of some drawing you saw in my bag? The whole idea is so far-fetched it's ridiculous. Preposterous. Oh, no. But I know why you're really here.'

His grey eyes studied her face. 'Why, then?'

Allie leaned back against the wall, the action stretching the material of her shirt taut across her firm breasts. Her voice growing husky, she said, 'You said it yourself; it's because you couldn't bear to think that you'd been stood up. Your pride wouldn't tolerate it. So you looked for some excuse to chase after me. Now, *that's* the truth, so why don't *you* admit it?'

To her surprise he nodded. 'Yes, I'll admit to that. I'm—*was*—greatly attracted to you. And I allowed myself to hope—but that turned out to be a mistake. You're not the kind of woman I thought you were.'

She gave a throaty chuckle. 'Do you know how pompous that sounds? And it's a lie in itself. You weren't looking for some kind of paragon. You were looking for a flesh-and-blood woman. The kind that had sexual attraction, who turned you on. You're as frustrated as hell and it shows.' Her voice rose. 'So don't try and make out that you were looking for something more than that. All you wanted was sex.'

She lifted a hand as Drake went to speak. 'Oh, OK, maybe you cloaked it in a little romance to help persuade me, even played at being cold to start with in the hope that I'd be intrigued. But the basic fact is that you saw me, wanted me, and set out to seduce me. It's as simple as that. And you thought you'd got me where you wanted me—panting to get into bed with you. And that's what this is all about. Don't try to deny it. You're just mad because I didn't stay around to deliver. That's what's really got to you. That's why you've come on this crazy chase after me.'

She paused, then said venomously, 'But you're wasting your time. For you this is just a wild-goose chase, because this is one goose who isn't going to come across.'

Drake didn't speak at first; he was thinking that in his experience when a woman got angry her features became sharp and shrewish, thoroughly nasty, and he'd thought the saying that a woman looked beautiful when she was angry to be downright nonsense. Until now. To Allie it brought a flush of colour that accen-

tuated her high cheekbones, and made her blue eyes
flash like sapphires. In repose she was an extremely
pretty girl, but when full of emotion like this she was
nothing less than excitingly, achingly lovely. Only it
was the wrong emotion. He wanted her hot with passion, not anger. Disappointment making his voice
sharp, he said, 'I'm not leaving here, Allie, so you
might as well accept it and make the best of it.'

'There is no best to it.' He merely shrugged and
she said sardonically, 'As I'm quite sure you saw
when you broke in earlier, there is only one bed—and
I certainly don't intend to share it, whatever lascivious
thoughts are going through your one-track mind.'

'There are plenty of pillows; I'll make myself comfortable on the armchairs.'

She gave a gasp at his audacity. 'It may have es-
caped your notice, but you haven't been invited to
stay.'

'Are you going to invite me?'

'No!'

'So now you know why I didn't ask.' He looked at
her balled fists and said more gently, 'You know,
you'd save yourself a lot of aggro if you'd just tell
me what you're up to. Maybe I could even help.'

Oh, sure, Allie jeered inwardly. I can just imagine
the kind of 'help' I'd get from you. You'd either adopt
a holier-than-thou attitude and go running to the
authorities, or else you'd take over and I'd be lucky
if I ended up with anything. So she just laughed and
said, 'You want to help me explore monasteries and
kremlins, to look round art galleries and museums? Is
that what you mean? Because that's all I'm doing.'

'You can protest all you like, Allie, but nothing you say will convince me that you're not up to something. Why won't you let me help you?'

She chose to be obtuse and gave an angry shrug. 'You know something, Drake? You're becoming extremely boring. But then, I'd already found that out in Moscow. The way you disapproved of my clothes, and the way you worried over me if I even tried to take a step alone at night—God, it was suffocating!'

Allie saw his face set and wondered if she had gone too far, but he must have been really thick-skinned because he merely said, 'Maybe I had cause.'

'Rubbish. You're just the type who likes to tyrannise over any woman, even a stranger.'

'But I didn't want you to be a stranger,' he pointed out.

She looked at him and it was suddenly between them again. The tension of frustrated desire, the hungry, aching need for fulfilment. Allie recognised that it went deep with him; it had to to make him come after her like this. But strangely she wasn't afraid. She had no fear that he would lose control and take her by force. Although he could quite easily. He was much, much stronger than she, and the house was set well apart from any other so that if she screamed it would not be heard. But Drake was too civilised for that; however much she pushed him she knew that he would never hurt her—not physically, at least. Emotionally, he already had.

'I don't want you to stay,' she repeated.

'I'm sorry, you don't have any choice.'

'If this was England I'd call the police and have you thrown out,' she threatened.

'But this is Russia—and there's no way you'd ever call the police because you don't want them or anyone else to know what you're up to. Do you?'

She gave a tired sigh and made to point out that he was wrong, but Drake forestalled her, saying urgently, 'Look, Allie, if you don't want to tell me then OK, I accept that. But the authorities here are hot on any foreigners who break the rules. You could be putting yourself at extreme risk. Before you go any further I want you to promise me that you'll think very hard about what you're contemplating. Please don't put yourself into danger. If you were caught the best that could happen would be that you'd be thrown out of the country.' He paused to lend emphasis to his words. 'The worst could be that you'd end up in a Russian prison.'

Allie stared at him, feeling suddenly afraid, a chill of apprehension running through her as for the first time she saw that maybe this wasn't just a wonderful adventure, but might have serious consequences. For a minute she thought about abandoning the whole idea, was even on the point of telling Drake all about it.

But then he said forcefully, 'I care about what happens to you, Allie. I care very much.'

He had seen the indecision in her face, had thought that he was winning, but then saw her stiffen at his last words and knew he had lost her. Drake gritted his teeth in anger, wondering why the thought of his caring for her should make her so anti. Had she been hurt in the past and no longer trusted men, or was it just that she was so career-minded that she didn't want to commit herself to a relationship that might risk her independence? In other words sex was OK, but that was as far as it went. He didn't want to think that. His original feeling about Allie was that she was straight and honest; it almost frightened him to think that he could have been wrong.

But she'd already admitted to lying to him and he saw now that he couldn't rely on his instinct, that he really didn't know her at all. Common sense told him to leave and let her get on with what she wanted to do, not to get involved. And if she got into trouble then it was her own fault. But a stubborn streak in him clung tenaciously to his first feelings on seeing her—she had made his stomach lurch and given him what might be a ray of hope in the mess of his life. For that feeling alone he would stay and try to keep her safe.

She gave him a derisive look, said, 'Oh, sure,' on a note of open disbelief, then turned away. 'I'm going to bed. You can wait outside while I get ready.'

He didn't argue but went outside and closed the door. Allie thought of bolting it but knew it wouldn't do any good; he would only bang on the door until she let him in. She washed as best she could in a bowl of water, put on her nightdress and climbed into the bed, which was surprisingly comfortable with a deep feather mattress and sheets that smelt of summer sun.

'OK, you can come in,' she called out, and resolutely turned her back as she heard Drake moving around, drawing the chairs together, making himself comfortable.

Turning out the lamp, he said, 'Goodnight, Allie.'

She didn't answer but lay awake, even though she was tired, her senses on edge, terribly aware even of the sound of his breathing. Suddenly she wished that things were different, that there weren't this great chasm between them. She felt hungry for Drake's arms around her, for him to hold her close. Angry with herself, Allie impatiently pushed these thoughts aside and concentrated instead on working out how she was going to get rid of him. But nothing came to mind before she fell asleep.

When he heard her breathing become even, Drake too slept, but he woke a few hours later, stiff and cramped by the confines of the chairs. Carefully and quietly he stood up and stretched, arching his back. He was wearing only his sleeping shorts but wasn't at all cold. Going to the window, he looked out at the silvered landscape, thinking of the strange circumstances that had brought him here. By rights he ought to be back in London taking up the reins of his job, picking up the social round, visiting Emma.

His mind came to an abrupt halt at the thought of his fiancée, and he was filled with a great sense of guilt. Resolutely he pushed her out of his mind, knowing there was no point in dwelling on it. But it made him turn and look at Allie, the moonlight from the window falling across her. He wondered what she would do if he went over and kissed her awake, got in bed beside her and started to make love to her.

Would she push him away and tell him to go to hell? Probably. But there was always the chance that she wouldn't. It rather depended on whether she was as cheap as she made out or whether he had been right on that night when they had first embraced and he had been convinced that she was as attracted to him as he to her.

There was, of course, only one way to find out. Drake walked across the room and reached out to touch her but then paused. In her sleep she had pushed the covers aside and he could see the swell of her breasts beneath the silk nightdress gently rising and falling as she breathed. The by now familiar ache of longing filled his loins, a hurt both agonising and pleasurable. But she looked so small in the wide bed, so innocent and vulnerable, her long lashes casting soft shadows across her cheeks, her blonde hair fallen across her forehead. The protective instinct he had felt towards her from the first reasserted itself even more fiercely. Drawing back, he went softly back to his makeshift bed and settled down again, trying to forget the torturing need and go back to sleep.

Allie woke with a pleasurable feeling the next morning. The sun was shining through the open window across her bed and she felt warm and luxurious in the softness of the mattress. Outside she could hear birds singing, a sound entirely new and wonderful. For a few relaxed moments she just revelled in her own senses, but then sat up with a jerk as she remembered that Drake was there. Only he wasn't. Not physically. The armchairs had been restored to their former position on either side of the pot-bellied iron stove and the pillows had been put away. For a second Allie thought it had all been a bad dream, but then saw his small case standing neatly out of the way against the wall. So he was still around.

Quickly she got out of bed, went to the bathroom and dressed, putting on a sun top and denim shorts, shoving her feet into a pair of espadrilles. Tugging a brush through her hair, she looked out of the window but could see no sign of Drake. The thought of just getting in the car and abandoning him began to grow. Cautiously she opened the door and looked out. Both cars were there, her own standing temptingly nearest to the track. She hadn't bothered to bring everything into the house; all she had to do was sling her few clothes into her bag and take off.

But Drake couldn't be far away, he would hear the car and come running, and it would be easy to follow the cloud of dust she would send up, so it would all be for nothing. Unless she could stop him following her. Allie looked at his Mercedes, wondering if she could put it out of action. A flat tyre would be easy but would only stop him for the length of time it would take him to change it. It would have to be two tyres at least. But that would take too long. There had to be an easier, quicker way.

Keeping her eyes open for Drake and at the same time trying to appear nonchalant, Allie strolled over to his car and tried the door. It was locked. Darn. She would have to try and get hold of his keys. Would he have taken them with him or left them in the house? The chances of him leaving them were remote but worth a try. There was still no sign of him. Going back into the house, Allie searched around the obvious places: table-top, windowsill, the shelf in the bathroom. Drake's shaving things were on the latter, in a neat sponge-bag, but there were no keys. His suitcase was unlocked. Feeling like a criminal, Allie knelt beside it as she opened it up. Clothes neatly folded. A couple of books, one of them in Russian. His passport—he wouldn't get far without that if she pinched it! But its loss wouldn't stop him from chasing her all over Russia itself, she realised as she replaced it.

She rummaged at the bottom of the case, found something else and brought it out. It was a photograph in a silver frame. Allie found herself looking at the girl who must be his fiancée. Long dark hair blowing around her head, the girl was laughing at the photographer, the radiance of happiness in her face. Her left hand was up, holding back her hair, and there was a ring on her engagement finger, so there could be no doubt. Allie imagined it being taken as a memento of the day they had become engaged, and felt an absurd stab of jealousy for the absolute certainty of shared love that shone from the girl.

Thrusting the photograph back with an almost angry movement, Allie made sure the contents of the case were as she'd found them before she put it back in its place.

So now what? She hunted round again, even moving her own things out of the way, then stopped suddenly as it occurred to her that Drake might have gone through her things as she had gone through his, looking for some clue to her own quest. But the little book was well hidden in the car and she didn't think that he would have found it; anyway he didn't know that it even existed. Frustrated, she went outside again and walked for a little way down the track, wondering whether to chance it and run. Then she saw Drake.

But this was Drake as she had never seen him before. He was standing at the edge of the lake and had obviously been swimming. Facing away from her, he was pausing while drying himself to watch a heron as it flew across the sky. He was wearing only a pair of boxer shorts that clung to his figure, his hair dishevelled from being vigorously rubbed dry, and water still glinting on his chest where the rising sun caught him. His body was lean and smooth, his chest not at all hairy. Allie hadn't expected him to be so muscular; people who worked inside at a desk year in and year out usually weren't, but Drake's shoulders were wide, his arms powerful, telling of contained strength, and there wasn't an ounce of fat on him.

Allie swallowed; her mouth had gone dry and her chest had tightened. She found that she wanted to be held in his arms again, to feel her body pressed against his. To run her hands over his chest. To be kissed.

As if feeling himself watched, Drake suddenly swung round to face her. For a long moment they just stared at each other, then Allie turned away and began to hurry blindly back to the house. But Drake came after her, called out, 'Allie! Wait!'

She didn't want to wait, she wanted to run, to leave temptation behind, along with a desire so strong it threatened to drown common sense. But she couldn't do that, so she slowed and let him catch up with her.

Drake's eyes searched her face but, after one quick glance, she kept hers averted. 'Allie?' He went to put his hands on her shoulders but she stepped back and he balled his hands into fists. 'Were you looking for me?'

'No.' Allie made the denial strongly but her heart was thumping too loud in her chest. 'I hoped you'd gone.'

His voice becoming soft, insinuating, Drake said, 'Look at me.'

'Why should I?'

'Because I think you're afraid to.'

She laughed, but, lifting her hand, Allie ran it through her hair, hiding her face. 'I don't think so.'

'So look at me,' he insisted.

Slowly she lifted her head and turned to stare at him, her skin strained tight with tension. 'What's the matter?' she taunted. 'Aren't I paying you enough attention? Are you so conceited, so narcissistic that you need to be continuously admired? OK, if that's what you want.' Deliberately she let her eyes run over him, stripping him, the same way men undressed a woman. She let her gaze, openly concupiscent, linger over his chest, then work its way down to where his wet shorts clung to him, leaving no doubt of his masculinity.

Suddenly Drake lifted his hand and caught her under the chin, lifting her face. His voice grating, he said, 'You wanton little she-devil. That wasn't what I meant and you know it.'

'Do I?' She laughed a challenge.

Drake swore under his breath, then, his tone fierce, unsteady, he said, 'I ought to throw you on the grass and take you here and now.'

'You wouldn't dare!'

His eyes narrowed, and Drake reached out to take hold of her. 'You know something, Allie? You really shouldn't throw out challenges like that unless you're prepared to have them taken up. But then, maybe that's what you want.'

Allie stood transfixed as he drew her towards him, not knowing whether to push him away or to let him do what her treacherous heart and body were definitely crying out for. He gazed down at her face, at her large, vulnerable eyes and moist lips, waiting for her to protest. But, although her breath was gasping and unsteady, she made no sound, just gazed up at him with a look half of fear, half of longing. With a great surge of excitement at her capitulation, Drake bent to kiss her—but just then a movement caught his eye and he glanced up.

A woman carrying a baby was hurrying along the track towards them. Breaking into a run, the woman cried out in Russian, 'Allie, are you all right?'

Cursing, Drake straightened as Allie whirled round. 'Ludmilla!'

'Is this man hurting you? Who is he?'

Before she could think of a reply, Drake put his hands on Allie's shoulders in a possessive gesture and said smoothly, 'Didn't Allie tell you I was joining her? I'm her husband.'

CHAPTER SIX

ALLIE gasped at the downright lie, and went to twist round and confront him. But Drake held her still with an iron grip and whispered urgently into her ear, 'For God's sake don't turn round.'

'What? But why...?' Her voice faded as she realised that Drake must have been taken over by his libido and hadn't yet managed to control it. And in those wet shorts he must be sight enough to make any woman blush. Allie was strongly tempted to pull away and see how he would handle the situation, but then her sense of the ridiculous took over and she began to giggle inwardly.

'Is this true, Allie?' Ludmilla asked suspiciously. 'You said nothing about your husband coming to join you here.'

Trying not to laugh aloud and to look innocent at the same time was extremely difficult. Her blue eyes dancing with mischief, Allie said, 'I didn't know myself.'

'But how did he know where to find you?'

Looking over her shoulder at Drake, Allie said, 'Yes, how did you know how to find me?' Now get out of that one, she thought triumphantly.

But Drake was quite equal to the challenge. His face and voice bland, he said, 'But don't you remem-

ber, *mayah lobof*? You called me on your mobile
phone.'

Outraged at being called his darling, in any language, Allie deliberately wrenched herself free and
stepped away from him, expecting to enjoy his dis-
comfiture. But when she glanced down from under
her lashes she saw that he was now completely in
control again. Drake gave her a mocking grin, guessing exactly what she was thinking, and there was such
devilment in his eyes that to her annoyance Allie
found she couldn't help but grin back.

Ludmilla was curious about Drake and stayed to
talk, but presently the baby began to cry and she went
back to her own house. By that time Allie had realised
how incongruous it was to be sharing anything with
Drake, especially laughter—and for such a provoca-
tive reason! It was a lapse, a lowering of the draw-
bridge that up to now had been firmly closed against
him. Determined to slam it shut in his face again, she
turned to go back to the dacha, but Drake fell into
step beside her, saying, 'Have you had breakfast yet?
Why don't I make us an omelette?'

Tauntingly, she said, 'How domesticated you
sound.'

'Oh, I am. I've been fully house-trained.'

'Really? Who by?' She spoke rather harshly and
waited, wondering if he would take the opening she'd
given him to tell the truth.

Drake's eyebrows rose at her tone. 'By my mother,
I suppose. But I've been looking after myself for a
long time and you tend to learn how to cope.'

So he'd ducked out, yet again. They reached the

dacha but Allie stayed outside, sitting on a wooden bench seat in the sun. He'd offered to cook, so let him.

'What shall we do today?' Drake called through the open doorway after a few minutes of the pleasant sound of eggs being beaten and the smell of frying bacon drifting appetisingly into the air.

'"We"? Since when has "we" been an option?'

Coming out, Drake put a mug of coffee into her hands, looked down at her for a minute, and then said, quite matter-of-factly for a world-shattering statement, 'Oh, from the moment we met, of course.' He watched her mouth fall open, gave a malicious grin, and said, 'Let's eat out here, shall we?'

Allie watched him broodingly as he brought out a cloth for the rustic table, cutlery, slices of thick bread spread with butter. It all seemed so normal, as if they were a couple, used to each other and content in each other's company. But then Drake glanced up and caught her watching him. He gave a slow, knowing smile that suddenly made her feel so sensuous inside, but not only that—it made her feel as if she was beautiful, an object of desire, and set her senses flaming with an inner fire. Shaken, she turned away, damning him for the effect he had on her, cursing her own wayward senses for betraying her like this.

Soon Drake brought out their breakfast and they ate in a silence that to Allie felt screamingly loud. But it seemed that Drake wasn't about to break it, so at length, feeling driven, she said curtly, 'There's supposed to be a museum of icons in a disused monastery not too far away; I thought I'd go and look round it.'

'Suits me fine,' Drake said equably.

'It wasn't an invitation.'

'All right. I'll just follow behind you, then.'

'Don't you ever listen? I said—'

'I know what you said,' Drake interrupted tersely. 'But you're the one who isn't listening. I told you last night that I'm not going to let you out of my sight. So why not stop messing around and tell me what you're up to?'

'Oh, for heaven's sake!' Allie angrily pushed her plate to one side.

Giving her a look that wasn't altogether unsympathetic, he said, 'You might as well make the best of it, Allie, because I'm here to stay.'

She walked moodily away, leaving him to clear up. The track climbed a slight rise to a grove of trees that overlooked the lake. It was already hot and she sat on the grass in the shade, wondering what to do. Drake's last words about making the best of him being there echoed in her mind. It seemed that she had little choice, because the darn man just wasn't going to go away. Which meant that she had somehow to dump him, but he would be expecting that and would be on the lookout for any move she might make. Unless she could catch him off his guard. Somehow lull him into a false sense of her acceptance of his being there. But how on earth, given that he was so wary of her, could she do that?

There was one very obvious way, of course. She could let him make love to her.

Allie wasn't sure what had put that treacherous thought into her head. She angrily pushed it aside as being out of the question. Completely. It didn't even come into the equation. She wasn't into using sex as a means to an end and definitely not as a weapon, as some women did. Sex should be for mutual pleasure, a way of physically enriching a relationship that was already close, that had gone beyond friendship. As she had thought her feelings for Drake had gone beyond just friendship. No, not thought, had *known* they had gone way beyond that.

Picking at a strand of tall grass, Allie agitatedly began to bend it between her fingers. One thing she was sure of; no matter how antagonistic she was towards him, she just knew that making love with Drake would definitely be a mutual pleasure. For a few moments she indulged herself in imagining what it would be like to go to bed with him, but then found her cheeks getting hot and somehow pushed the thoughts aside. She was getting as frustrated as Drake had been earlier. The remembrance of that made her grin, and so she was smiling when Drake walked up the hill to join her.

Dropping down beside her and leaning on his elbow, he said, 'You have the most wonderful smile. I hope you were thinking about me.'

As she met his eyes, the smile faded, but then came back again, although this time brittle, false. 'Of course. Who else?' Her voice brisk, Allie said, 'I've decided to forgive you for following me and let you come with me to the monastery to see the icons.'

She went to get to her feet but Drake caught her wrist. 'Why the sudden change of heart?'

'You just told me to make the best of your being

here,' she pointed out. 'I don't want you with me, I wanted to be alone, but if I can't have that...' She shrugged. 'As you can't seem to get it into your head that I'm not interested in you, I suppose I'll have to put up with you. You can earn your keep by doing the driving.'

'Fair enough.' Drake rose easily but kept hold of her hand and pulled her up after him. He had changed out of his wet swimming trunks and had on jeans and an open shirt. Softly he said, 'But somehow I'm not convinced that you're not interested.'

She stiffened, said curtly, 'You'd better believe it, because it's true.'

'You say that a lot. Maybe you're trying to convince yourself and not me.'

Lifting her hand, she put it against his chest and pushed him away. 'In your dreams!' And she started walking briskly back to the house. There they collected Allie's bag and stuff that they might need for the day. She said, 'We'll take my car,' and, giving him no time to argue, she got into the passenger seat and waited for him to join her.

'If we used my car we could hand yours in and save some money,' he pointed out.

She saw through that ploy and said coldly, 'I prefer to be independent.'

Drake gave a smiling sigh. 'So I've noticed.'

It was some way to the museum and took them over half an hour, Allie reading the map and giving directions. 'It shouldn't be too far now. See, there are the domes. Oh, how wonderful, they're red. Can you imagine an English church with a red-painted spire? The parishioners would have a fit.'

With an appreciative grin, Drake said, 'The Russians love colour; all their traditional costumes are full of it, especially red.'

'Because they were communists?'

'No! The word *krasniy* used to mean beautiful as well as red. Red Square in Moscow means beautiful or magnificent square; it has nothing to do with communism. And in the dacha—you know that corner where the red embroideries are and the icon is on the wall? Well, that's the sacred part of the house where you go to pray or where the men sit and talk when there are decisions to be made.'

'Really? I never knew that. Great-Gran—' She stopped abruptly. 'We take the next right, just there at the roundabout.'

For a few moments there was a mess of traffic as a tourist coach tried to turn into the same street but was held up by a colourful horse and cart that was giving rides to children. Thankfully Drake had to give the road all his attention and she thought he might have missed her slip of the tongue. Allie cursed herself for having made it, but it was so easy to forget oneself when with Drake. His manners were so easy and—when they weren't fighting—she felt so companionable with him that it was easy to forget that she had to be constantly on her guard—for more reasons than one. She was tense for a while but as he made no mention of it after they'd parked and walked into the museum Allie gradually began to relax.

There were lots of icons to see and they were all

beautiful, but there was only so much magnificence she could assimilate in one go, and after an hour or so they wandered out into the sunlight again. There was a park nearby that followed a meandering stream with a little waterfall. The beds were full of flowers and there was a drone of bees in the still air. In the middle of the park there was the usual iron statue of Lenin, pointing. He always seemed to be pointing, although Allie had noticed it was often in different directions.

'Where was he pointing to?' she asked as they sat on a seat that overlooked the waterfall.

'To a rosy future.'

Allie lifted her head and laughed. 'No wonder he didn't know which way.'

The sun was on her face and the clean line of her throat; it made her hair, already fair, glint like spun gold, and her eyes the clear aquamarine of the sky. Unable to resist, Drake lifted a hand and gently touched her cheek with the backs of his fingers. 'When are you going to let me kiss you again?'

'Read my lips.' And she mouthed, 'Never.'

But the second syllable made her lips pucker deliciously and Drake leant forward to kiss them. Allie pulled indignantly away and he raised his eyebrows. 'Didn't you say now?'

Her eyes narrowed. 'You are a cheat and a hypocrite, you know that?'

'A cheat? OK, I know you said never. I admit it. But a hypocrite? What have I done to make you call me that?'

His deviousness both angered and appalled her. She

could have given herself to this man, believing that he really cared about her, that she meant something to him. As he had led her to believe, as he was still trying to make her believe. But what a dishonest act it would have been on his part. To have sex together, the sort of sex where two people met, had mutual pleasure in the act, and then went their separate ways, their emotions still intact, was at least straight and honest. But where one deceived the other into thinking that emotions were involved, that this was a physical commitment to love, then there was *nothing* more hypocritical. All she could do was thank her stars that she had found out about his duplicity in time.

'Oh, for heaven's sake!' She stood up and strode back through the park, her mind, as always, on the problem of how to be rid of him. The answer came when she was least prepared for it, so unexpectedly that she almost didn't see the opportunity and take advantage of it.

They had gone to a café for lunch and then into a big tourist bazaar where there were many stalls of traditional wares: malachite bracelets and necklaces, dark green and heavy; lots of jewellery made of amber in which you could see the dark traces of petrified insects when you held it up to the light; hundreds of babushka dolls in all shapes, colours and sizes; beautiful dolls in traditional costumes. The variety and ingenuity of the craftsmen and artists seemed endless. Allie strolled along the stalls, stopping to touch, to admire, the typical tourist, with Drake always beside her. She bought some delicately embroidered handkerchiefs for her mother, a set of dolls for a friend's child, then stopped to pick up a gorgeous amber neck-lace, each stone delicately carved. 'Oh, how lovely.' She looked at the price, knew that she could bargain to try and cut it down, but it was still too much. With a regretful smile for the stall-holder she turned away.

'I think I might get something here for my mother,' Drake remarked.

'OK.' Allie moved on down the row of stalls, near-ing the exit.

Drake glanced in her direction but didn't feel any alarm, knowing that she couldn't get anywhere with-out him because he had the keys to the car in his pocket. He made his purchase and went to move on, but hadn't got very far before the stall-holder urgently called him back. 'Please, one of these notes is torn; I cannot take it.'

He went back, tried to find a better note of that value in his wallet but didn't have one, so it meant starting the whole transaction again.

Allie had heard the woman call him and glanced over her shoulder as she examined some wooden thimbles, then felt the hairs on the back of her neck stand on end as she realised that here might be a chance. Within seconds she was out of the building and haring back to the car, pulling the spare set of keys she'd been given out of her bag as she ran. People stared as she tore down the road, dodging pe-destrians and jumping down into the road from the pavement to make better time, then leaping out of the way as a car came round the corner. She erupted into the big square where she was sure they had parked, but for a dreadful moment couldn't see the car. Had she come the wrong way? Were they parked in a different square?

But then she ran past a tour bus and there it was, hidden in its shadow. With a sob of thankfulness she unlocked the door and jumped in. Allie's hands were trembling and she had to grit her teeth and force herself to calm down before she could get the key in the ignition and start the engine. She reversed out fast, causing another car to honk angrily, but then she was on her way, driving out of the square in whatever direction was quickest.

The children's pony cart came trundling along, bringing everyone to a halt. Allie looked anxiously out of the window and nearly died as she saw Drake run out of the street from the bazaar. But there was no way he could catch her, if only the road would clear. There were no taxis around and it would take him an age to hire a car. But if he caught her before she got out of this darn traffic jam... At that moment he turned his head, saw her, and began to pelt up the street. Allie gave a whimper of fear and, too desperate to wait, pulled out of the queue. Swerving round the back of the cart with inches to spare, the furious yells of the driver in her ears, she put her foot on the accelerator and tore down the road as if all the devils of hell were after her.

Only when she was well away from the square did Allie slow down to a reasonable speed and start to think ahead. It had all happened so suddenly, an opportunity seized, that there had been no time to plan, or to look at the map. She tried to put herself in Drake's place. What would he do? Hire a car and

come after her to the dacha, she supposed. But Allie
had no intention of going back there. She had unpacked only a few clothes and toiletries, which could
easily be replaced. But it was a nuisance because the
dacha was in the area where she wanted to be. Now
she would have to make a huge circle round and come
at the place from the east instead of the west, which
would make the exact spot harder to find. And at the
moment she was going in entirely the wrong direction.
But not to worry; she would do it. The most important
thing was that she had got away from Drake, and the
next was to make absolutely sure he didn't find her
again. Which would mean exchanging the car for another. Darn!

Leaving the outskirts of the town, she put her foot
down, looking for somewhere she could turn off and
lose herself, but the road went on in a depressing line,
as straight as any ancient Roman road. For the fiftieth
time she glanced in the rear mirror and gave a sigh
of relief. No car behind her, only a couple of distant
specks that could be bicycles, although she didn't remember having overtaken any. A signpost came into
view and she slowed to translate the Cyrillic lettering,
recognising the name of a distant town. Good, she'd
head for there, and do a big half-circle. The turning
was half a mile further on. Allie automatically glanced
in her mirror again as she indicated to turn left across
the carriageway. The specks were larger and she saw
they were motorbikes, one far ahead of the other.

A feeling of uneasiness gripped her and she swung
into the side turning with a squeal of brakes and tyres,
then put her foot down, her eyes on the mirror. The

first bike was following her. With the certainty of
dread, Allie knew that it was Drake.

Driving faster than she had ever done in her life,
Allie tore along the road. Luckily there was little or
no traffic to hold her up. She swooped past a couple
of Russian Ladas as if they didn't exist, her engine
groaning, but the empty road gave Drake the chance
to go fast too. The bike came close behind and her
heart sank as she saw that the low-slung silver and
black machine was big and powerful. There was no
way she could hope to outrun it. It drew alongside
and one glance confirmed her worst fears. Drake was
crouched low over the handlebars, goggles over his
eyes, but without a helmet or any protective clothing,
his hair blowing back from his head. Fleetingly Allie
wondered how on earth he had managed to get hold
of it—and so quickly. She hoped he'd stolen it and
would get arrested. Serve him right! He waved to her
to stop and when she ignored him drew ahead,
swerved in front of her and started to slow down.
Allie tried to go round him but he was looking back
over his shoulder and went in front of her again.

Cursing, she changed gear, wiggled the car from
side to side to try and divert him, but she knew it was
no use; even if she managed to get past him he could
easily overtake her again. So maybe it was time to try
another tactic. She stopped. Drake saw and turned the
bike in a circle, came to a halt with his front wheel
touching her front bumper. For a minute they just sat
and stared at one another, Allie in fury, Drake with a
wary but determined thrust to his jaw. She waited for
him to get off the bike, to come to the car. She was

already in reverse gear, all ready to let out the clutch
and get away again, and if she knocked over the bike
in the process, then so much the better. He'd taken
the bike; let him do the explaining.

But Drake didn't get off the bike; instead he
seemed to be waiting. Too late, Allie remembered the
other motorbike. It came up and Drake waved to the
driver to go behind her. With mounting fury, Allie
realised that she was trapped between the two.

There were two men on the second bike. One of
them got off and went up to Drake, looking curiously
at Allie as he passed. Drake handed the bike to him,
swinging himself easily off the powerful machine,
then walked over to the car and opened the driver's
door.

'Turn off the engine,' he ordered.

Allie gave him a smouldering look. 'Go to hell!'

Reaching past her, he turned it off himself and
pocketed the keys. Then he went to speak to the two
motorcyclists. Allie saw some money passed over,
hands were shaken, and the two young men, grinning
widely, one of them even having the cheek to wave
at her derisively as he passed, roared away.

Coming back to the car, Drake said curtly, 'Move
over.'

She glared at him but did as he asked, or rather
commanded.

'Nice try,' he commented as he sat beside her.
Starting the car, he drove on, not stopping until they
were back at the dacha.

Allie spent the journey sitting in simmering silence.
As soon as they pulled up outside the little wooden

house she went to get out of the car, but Drake stopped her. His face tense, he said, 'I know what you're thinking—that you almost made it this time and that next time you will. Well, you can forget it. I'm going to be as close to you as a shadow. You won't *get* another chance. I'll make damn sure of that.'

Her flashing eyes annihilated him. '*Why* are you doing this?'

Drake gave a short laugh. 'Someone has to save you from your own stupidity.'

The anger and hostility in her eyes intensified. 'I hate you! I hate you with the deepest loathing I have ever felt in my life!' And then she swung out of the car and ran up the hill to the grove of trees.

Drake left her there for over an hour, giving her rage a chance to die down, although he was pretty certain that she would still spit at him like a wildcat no matter how long he left her. Carrying two cans of cola, he strolled up the hill and sat down on the grass beside her. 'Cola? They're quite cold; I've been cooling them off in the lake.'

Allie just glowered at him and folded her arms across her chest, turning to glare at the innocent lake instead.

Apparently not at all put out, Drake put a can down by her side and then opened his own. Lifting it, he took a long swallow, his throat working. Allie gave him a quick glance and then licked lips gone suddenly dry. She was thirsty, had known that she couldn't stay up here indefinitely, but seeing him drink, the long column of his neck, his shirt tight across his chest as he arched, had made her feel even drier. And her chest felt tight too. Biting her lip, she looked away, determined not to even look at him again, let alone speak to him.

But then he completely devastated her by saying, 'Tell me, Allie, which of your great-grandparents was it that came from Russia?'

She swung round, her face full of horror. 'How did you—?' But then she stopped abruptly, remembering her slip of the tongue earlier that day. So he had noticed, after all. She ought to have known he would; he was too alert not to, and too intelligent not to put two and two together and come up immediately with the right answer. Her face full of chagrin, she said, 'Mind your own damn business.'

'Well, I suppose I ought to thank you for not trying to pretend you don't know what I mean.' She didn't speak and he said, 'You might as well tell me all about it, you know. You're going to have to tell me some time, and it might as well be now.'

With one furious movement, Allie pushed herself to her feet. 'Why the hell should I tell you anything? Just what gives you the right to think that you can just walk into my life and follow me and watch me and interrogate me like some damn prison guard? We went out together a few times in Moscow—and that was it! You're nothing to me and I don't want to even know you. Just go away and leave me alone!' she yelled at him furiously.

'Liar!' Drake came to his feet so swiftly that she fell back a startled step. 'You're not indifferent to me. You're just so obsessed with this crazy quest you're on that you won't even allow yourself to think about your own emotions, your own needs.'

'I certainly don't *need* you!'

'No? I wonder why I don't believe you?'

'God, don't you ever listen? I hate and despise you!' She was glaring at him, her face white with anger, her hands balled into fighting fists as if she'd like to hit him.

'Tell me, Allie; why all this argument? Why all this constant denial? Maybe it's because you're afraid to let yourself show your real feelings. Maybe it's a subconscious way of trying to force me into taking you. Is that what you want? Are you so afraid to let go of your inhibitions that you want me to take them from you?'

She gasped, stunned by his accusation. 'Me? Inhibited? You must be mad. No, it's you. If you hadn't—' Allie came to an abrupt stop. She had been about to fling his fiancée in his face when it suddenly occurred to her that to do so would reveal how hurt she had been by his deception. And she had too much pride for that.

'If I hadn't what?' Drake took hold of her arm, urgent for her to finish what she had been about to say, instinctively knowing that it had been important, that it could have explained all the problems between them, maybe even have solved them.

A bleak look came into Allie's eyes and she shook her head, her face tightening in rejection. 'If you hadn't been so egotistical, so certain that no woman could ever think you anything but God's gift, and had just let me leave Moscow in peace, then we wouldn't be in this stupid mess.'

She had covered well, but Drake was certain it wasn't what she had been going to say, the true explanation she had been about to blurt out in the heat of anger. His voice edged with disappointment, he said curtly, 'The mess could be cleared up in two minutes if only you'd confide in me.'

'People only confide in someone they trust.'

He found that the criticism hurt, which made him impatient with her. 'But why won't you trust me? I mean you no harm—quite the opposite; you should know that by now.'

'Oh, for heaven's sake.' Allie made an irritated gesture. 'What makes you think I want you around to—to protect me, or whatever it is you think you're doing? I'm a grown woman and I can handle my own life. I don't want some man watching over me like a guardian angel. I want to take care of myself, to be free to make my own decisions, do as I want and go where I want.'

Some part of his mind, the part that was always being hammered at by liberated women in the media, told him that if women wanted to be independent then they should be able to take the consequences, but the basic masculine part of him knew that this was no time or place for such an indulgence. If there was ever any place for it at all. He could, on a hypothetical level, admire her attitude. In reality he hated every word of it, undermining as it did the basic principles of gender. As it was, she had pushed him into a corner, a no-win situation whichever way he answered.

Ambiguously, he said, 'This is hardly a situation you come across in the normal course of life.' Sitting down again, he picked up his can, then held the other one up to her. 'Come on,' he coaxed. 'Come and sit down and have a drink. We'll talk about something else. Something mundane. Anything but what's really on our minds. OK? We're English; we ought to be able to talk about the weather for at least an hour.'

Allie smiled a little at that, hesitated, but then dropped down beside him and took the cola. It had been shaken up and the cold liquid spat at her as she opened it, making her lick it off the back of her hand. Glancing up, she saw that Drake was watching her, his eyes suddenly dark.

'Don't!' she exclaimed. 'Don't look at me like that.'

'Like what?'

'You know. As if—as if you want me.'

'I do want you. You know that.'

'But you don't have to damn well show it all the time, do you? It makes me—' She broke off, biting her lip. 'Just don't look at me like that.'

Drake gritted his teeth for a second, but then said, 'I'm sorry. But I can't help the way I feel about you. But as you've expressed your disapproval I'll try not to notice that you're a very attractive woman. I'll try not to think that when you licked your hand just now I wished it was me that was licking your skin. I'll try not to see how damn sexy you are. I might even try to sleep at night instead of lying awake wishing—' He stopped precipitately, gave a bitter smile. 'I'll just try to stop wishing.'

For a moment she was shaken by his vehemence, by the apparent sincerity of his outburst. But then Allie remembered how taken in she'd been by him, back in Moscow, and her heart hardened. 'Is that supposed to make me feel sorry for you? Well, I don't. If you don't like the situation, you can always leave.'

'Yeah, yeah.' He sounded fed up, suddenly tired.

They sat in silence for a while, finishing their drinks, then Allie felt somehow compelled to say, 'You don't know what it's like for a woman who wants to succeed in her career. Especially if you're short.'

'Short?' He gave her a half-amused, half-disbelieving look. 'You're kidding.'

'No, I'm not. If you think of a high-powered businesswoman, what image comes into your mind? Well? Go on, tell me.'

'OK.' Drake closed his eyes and then described the picture in his imagination. 'Very self-controlled. Perhaps a bit hard, tough, clever.'

'But what does she look like?'

'Always power-dressed in tailored suits, but good, expensive clothes. Hair well cut but easy to manage. High heels. Slim.' Opening his eyes, he nodded. 'And tall. Yes, you're right, I always think of career women as tall.'

'You see,' she said triumphantly. 'Nobody takes you seriously when they have to look down on you all the time. Even other, taller women. I'm fighting heightism, chauvinism, and every other "ism" that fate throws at you. Do you know what men usually say to me when they find out I'm a photographer and computer programmer? They say, ''What's a cute little thing like you doing in a job like that?'' It makes me want to scream.'

'Not all men are so patronising,' Drake pointed out.

'And you're not? I wonder why I don't believe that?'

Drake gave her a steady look. 'No, I'm not going to let you accuse me of that. Have I tried to tell you how to do your job?'

'No,' she admitted. 'But—'

'I know what you're going to say, where all this is heading. That I won't leave you alone. But this is nothing to do with your career.'

'It's to do with my life. I've learnt to stand on my own two feet. I don't need anyone to nursemaid me, protect me.'

'We're never going to agree on that, Allie. So long as you're in Russia, then you're stuck with me.'

Without another word, she stood up and strode back to the house, stony-faced. After a moment Drake got up and followed her.

It grew dark but the heat didn't let up. Lying in the bed tucked into the corner that night, Allie felt stifled by the heat and unable to sleep. They had eaten supper, perforce together, but Allie had refused to talk to him, and had left Drake to clear up while she had changed for bed. Then she had resolutely turned her back and ignored him when he'd wished her goodnight. Restlessly she tried to think of some other way of escape but her mind kept wandering back to Drake, until she angrily brought herself back to the eternal problem.

She tossed in discomfort; she was burning up; there was no air. Allie pummelled the pillow, which felt like a mound of bricks, and tried to settle, hoping that the night would get cooler as it progressed. It was difficult to tell whether or not Drake was asleep; she tried to listen for his breathing and occasionally heard him move on his makeshift bed, trying to get comfortable. But he might have done that in his sleep.

Allie pushed at the hair that clung damply to her forehead. To hell with it; she couldn't stand this any longer. As quietly as she could, she slipped out of bed and pushed her feet into her espadrilles, then crept towards the door.

'Going somewhere?'

Drake's voice in the darkness made her jump. After a moment she said shortly, 'I'm hot. I'm going outside to try to cool off.' And, without waiting for him to reply, she went out of the door.

Outside it didn't seem much cooler than in the house. The air was very still, without a breath of wind to stir the grass or the leaves on the trees. Somewhere a night bird called, the note sweet and clear. For a few moments she stood and listened, then slowly walked along the track towards the lake. There was no one around to see her in her nightdress, and that in itself felt strangely liberating. Allie felt suddenly adventurous, as one did when experiencing something for the first time. She became more aware of the sounds of the night—of the plop of water as a fish rose to the surface of the lake, of the swish of wings as a bird, disturbed by her passing, flew to a safer perch. Allie glanced back at the dacha to see if Drake had followed her, but could see no sign of him. But then he had no need to fear that she would try to escape; he had all the keys to both cars, and she was hardly likely to make a run for it dressed as she was.

The surface of the lake glistened like molten silver in the moonlight, ripples drifting softly to the bank. It looked very cool, very inviting. Going to the edge, Allie kicked off her shoes, poked her toe in and it felt delicious. She took another look round, tempted to undress completely, but then decided against it. There was a shelving, sandy slope to the river and it felt pleasant under her feet as she waded in, the water rising slowly up, bringing coolness at last to her heated skin. When it came up to her waist, Allie stopped for a moment to splash water onto her chest, then cupped her hands and let the beautifully cold water run down her face and throat. She gave a low murmur of sybaritic pleasure; it seemed as if it had been the first time she had felt really cool in days. Closing her eyes, she trickled the water over herself again, letting her wet hands slide down from her throat over her breasts. It felt so good, so good.

Subconscious awareness that she was being watched made her turn and look at the bank. Drake was there. She supposed she should have known that he would follow her. His face was very tense, all planes sharpened into chiselled hardness by the moonlight. For a moment they just stared at each other, until Allie turned away. Lowering herself into the depths of the lake, she began lazily to swim.

She didn't know when Drake came up beside her;
she had heard no splash, hadn't felt any disturbance
in the water, but suddenly he was there, swimming
with easy grace. She paused for a moment, then
turned onto her back so that she could look up at the
stars as she floated. It was a different sky with new
stars, new constellations, the air fresh and clear in this
unpolluted landscape. 'It's so incredibly beautiful,'
she whispered in awe.

'We're privileged,' Drake agreed softly in instant
understanding as he, too, turned onto his back.

They floated on the water for some time, gazing
their fill at the sky, making small movements with
hands and feet to keep themselves buoyant. Allie supposed she should have told him to go away, made
him leave her so that she could enjoy this moment
alone, but somehow the night was just too perfect to
feel anger or hate. She felt too small, too transient
under that immense mantle of velvet sky and stars.

Drake took her hand and for a moment she resisted,
but he murmured, 'Trees,' and she let him draw her
away from the overhanging branches. But once clear
he kept hold of her hand.

They came to where the bottom shelved towards
the shore and stood up, the water coming to above
Allie's waist, but much lower on Drake. He still held
her hand and stopped her when she went to get out.
'No. Wait.' His eyes intense, he let them run over her.
The wet silk clung to her like a transparent skin
moulded to her own. The skirt had floated up and gave
tantalising glimpses of her thighs. His voice thick with
emotion, Drake said, 'I have never seen anything as

beautiful as the sight of you standing in the water, cooling yourself. You looked like a water-nymph, a naiad, a creature too fragile and beautiful to be of this world. I expected you to disappear, to be a figment of my imagination. A dream from which I would wake.'

The night had already weaved its spell, but his words, spoken with such soft intensity, only added to the magic. Allie felt as if she was still floating, as if all her senses had surrendered to the wonderful peace and stillness. 'But I'm real,' she whispered.

'Too real,' he agreed. 'Too beautiful.'

There was bleakness in his voice and she was suddenly filled with deep tenderness towards him. The anger was gone and there was only the certain knowledge of how much she cared for him. Nothing else mattered, only that. She had been a fool to let anything get in its way, she could see that now. But it wasn't too late. Dreams could still come true. Leaning forward, Allie placed her lips against his for a second, then drew away.

Drake shuddered in awakened sensuality, taking instant fire from her kiss. He gasped, his body suddenly alive with tension. He gazed at her in wonder, overwhelmed by what the kiss had promised, then slowly lifted his hands to her shoulders. For a moment his eyes were riveted on her face, then he lowered his gaze to look again at her body. Slowly, with infinite pleasure and gentleness, he let his hands move down her throat to her breasts, his fingers trails of fire across her skin.

Allie gave a long, moaning sigh and moved sensuously beneath his hands. The sound, and the tremor of arousal that ran through her, excited him like a strong aphrodisiac. Drawing her closer, Drake caressed her hungrily, watching her face in the moonlight, feeling triumph when her lips parted and she frowned and gasped as his hands toyed with her nipples. He squeezed them gently, rubbing his thumbs around the growing buds, teasing them into tingling, overwhelming sensuality. Her eyes fluttered open, but then another wave of delight hit her and she closed them again, her head thrown back, neck arched, moving in abandoned pleasure in this wonderful game he was playing with her senses.

Suddenly it was too much. With a small cry Allie put her hands on his shoulders and pulled herself against him. He shuddered as he felt her against his chest, the slipperiness of the wet silk, the pressure of her breasts, the nipples surprisingly hard, but oh, God, how wonderfully erotic. He had needed nothing more to turn him on, but the feel of her against him at that moment was the most sensuous experience he had ever known. Half lifting her out of the water, Drake held her against his length. She was shorter than any woman he had ever been with and for their thighs to touch he had to hold her off her feet, but then he could press her close, let her feel how much he wanted her. He was so hard he made her gasp, but he liked that. He wanted her to know that she was going to be well and truly loved, was determined that their first night together would be one she would never forget, would look back on in awe of his virility.

With one hand behind her head he kissed her, letting passion run loose, his breath becoming a panting moan as she returned the embrace avidly, her mouth opening under his. But then she was almost biting his lips as she put her hands on either side of his head and rained small, moaning, almost desperate kisses on his mouth and throat. Drake gave a great groan and held her closer yet, only the thin, wet material of their clothes between them. He began to shake with panting anticipation, and cried out her name, the repressed hunger of the past week now wild and abandoned. Stooping, he picked her up in his arms and waded to the bank, but had to stop several times because Allie was kissing him again, so fiercely that he couldn't see. The joy of it when he thought he had lost her, the building excitement, the anticipation, was almost more than his body and senses could take.

It had been so long since his body had been awakened like this. So long since he had wanted sex so desperately. 'Allie. Oh, dear God, my darling. I can't see where I'm going. Stop for just a moment. Just till we get back to the house,' he pleaded.

But she laughed against his mouth, said only half in jest, 'No, I'm never going to stop. I'm going to kiss you like this—' she found his earlobe '—and like this—' her lips climbed his throat '—and like this, always like this.' And she returned to his mouth with raging hunger.

He accepted and returned it with a kind of sexual fury, then stumbled up the bank, and carried her barefoot through the grass, mumbling her name against her lips. 'I'm going to love you. God, how I'm going to love you.'

'How? How are you going to love me?' The question was a breathless sigh of excitement.

'Till you beg me to stop. Till you can't take any more.'

Allie chuckled against his mouth. 'It might be the other way round.'

He almost reeled at the thoughts that brought to his mind, to his quivering senses. Drake reached the dacha and shouldered open the door, kicked it shut behind him. Then he set her down, but immediately she was close to him again, running her hands over his chest, his arms, kissing the tiny nipples on his chest. Drake cried out and crushed her to him, held her there for a moment, but then, hands trembling, he held her a little away from him and looked steadily into her face. 'Allie, I want you to know that this—this isn't just sex. I care about you very deeply. You mean so much to me—have from the first. Do you understand what I'm saying, my darling?'

She gazed at him, filled with an inner joy and wonder that reached her heart, her soul. 'Oh, Drake.' Reaching up, Allie touched his face, wanting to hold this moment for ever.

But then Drake gave a wicked grin and drew her close again. 'But it's definitely about sex, too.'

Allie smiled, moved her body against his, felt his hard arousal, and chuckled with delicious pleasure. 'I somehow thought it might be.'

His eyes intent again, Drake pushed the straps of the nightdress off her shoulders, slowly peeled it off her. It had hidden nothing, but even so it had been a barrier between his eyes and her nakedness. As it

dropped to her ankles he gave a sigh of delight.
'You're so beautiful. So perfect.' He bent to kiss her,
his mouth hot against her throat, her breasts.

He would have gone on kissing her, but she said
softly, 'Wait,' and reached to take off his wet shorts,
deliberately touching him as she did so. He became
rigid under her hand, his whole body suspended in the
ecstasy of it, but then she moved away as she lifted
his shorts over him and let them fall. Drake sighed,
went down on his knees to kiss her.

Gasping, writhing, she cried out his name, then
pulled him to his feet as she said urgently, 'Please.
Please.'

Lifting her, he laid her on the bed and kissed her,
then said, 'A moment, my sweet. I'll be back in a
moment.' And he went to the bathroom.

But she couldn't just lie there and wait. Her heart
was singing with happiness and excitement. She knew
that this was right, that she loved him. What had gone
before didn't matter; it could all be sorted out. But
Allie had a feeling of guilt because she hadn't trusted
him, and she didn't want that. She wanted to start all
over again. Most of all she wanted to show him that
she'd been wrong, prove to him that she completely
loved and trusted him now. The love she could show
by giving herself to him, but the trust...? An idea
suddenly came to her; her trust could be proved if she
told him about her quest, showed him the little book
that her great-grandmother had left her. Exhilarated
by the idea, Allie decided to get the book, safely hidden away in the car, now, at once. To present him
with both proofs of her feelings and make the night

perfect. Too full of happiness to think further, Allie slid from the bed and went to where Drake's jeans hung on the back of a chair. Feeling in his pockets, she gave a little laugh of satisfaction as she found the keys.

But then Drake's voice, harsh with bitterness, came from behind her. 'I suppose I should have known.'

She turned, ready to smile and tell him of the gift she was about to make him. But the smile died as she saw the furious anger in his face, and she suddenly realised how it must look.

'What was the idea?' he asked with a snarl. 'To wear me out and then run off when I was asleep? You should have waited till then—but you just couldn't bear to let slip the opportunity to get hold of the keys, could you?'

CHAPTER SEVEN

FOR a moment Allie stared at Drake in appalled dismay, then said urgently, persuasively, 'But it isn't like that. I was going to get something from the car to give to you. I—'

She broke off as Drake suddenly surged forward and caught hold of her wrist, snatching the keys from her hand. Dangling them in front of her face, he yelled, 'Don't lie to me, you little bitch! Don't compound what you've done by yet more lies.'

'But I'm not! I wasn't...' Allie put her hands on his chest, feeling completely devastated. 'Please listen to me. I—'

But Drake pushed her roughly away. With an oath, he flung the keys across the room, then strode to his clothes and started dragging them on. Picking up one of his shirts, he threw it at her. 'Here, put this on. There's no point in flaunting your nakedness any longer. Your clever seduction scenario was spoilt by your own impatience.'

Holding the shirt bunched in front of her, knowing that everything had gone wrong, Allie said with a sob of dazed sorrow and bewilderment, 'But I didn't set out to seduce you. It just happened. I realised that I'd been wrong. That I could trust you. That's why I was going out to the car; I wanted to get the book my great-grandmother left me. I was going to tell you everything about—'

She broke off abruptly, her face whitening, as Drake laughed in open disbelief. 'What a very convenient excuse. How amazing that this revelation occurred to you at just the right moment.' Sarcasm gave way to anger again as he said savagely, 'You little liar. You care nothing for me. I doubt if you've ever cared about any man. And I'll never know why the hell I was fool enough to care about you. I must have been mad. Crazy. Well, OK. If you can go to these lengths, to actually prostitute yourself—'

'I didn't!' Allie's shocked voice interrupted him, but he ignored her.

'If this project you've undertaken means so much to you that you're willing to do *anything*—and I mean anything—to see it through, then I'm not going to stand in your way any longer. You can go to hell in your own sweet way.' He glared at her. 'Maybe you're there already.'

Her hands shaking, Allie put on his shirt, pulled it across her and tried to do up the buttons, but found that she couldn't. Her voice breaking, she said, 'Drake. I know how it seems, but I wasn't trying to run away again. I swear it. You've got to believe me.'

'Why the hell should I? You've done nothing but lie to me, probably from the first moment we met. You've even lied to your boss and your own family. But quite frankly I don't care any more.'

'But you must. Please. I—'

'No!' Drake suddenly turned on her, his face thunderous. 'Just shut up, will you? I tell you, I've had

enough. Do what you like. I don't damn well care.'
Picking up a couple of pillows, he headed for the
door.

'Where are you going?'

'To sleep in my car.' He fished in his pocket, found
the spare set of keys for her car and flung it on the
table. 'If you want to leave, go ahead. I'm certainly
not going to stop you.' He felt something else in his
pocket and pulled it out, dropped the paper-wrapped
object on the table beside the keys. 'And you might
as well have this.'

He went out, slamming the door behind him. Allie
stood frozen in dismay, then slowly walked over to
the table and unwrapped the parcel. Inside was the
amber necklace that she had admired in the bazaar. It
was what Drake must have been buying when she'd
taken the opportunity to try and escape from him. He
had meant it as a present for her all along. Looking
at it, letting the cold stone slide through her fingers,
Allie felt absolutely devastated. How could what she
thought was going to be the most sincere proof of her
love for him have rebounded on her like this? All
she'd wanted was to take him completely into her
confidence. But it had all turned out to be such a fi-
asco. For a while she couldn't believe that it had happened, was sure that soon he would realise how wrong
he'd been and come back into the dacha to apologise.
He couldn't have meant what he'd said; he must
surely care.

Outside, Drake put down the back seats of the car and
made himself as comfortable as he could. Not that he

would get any sleep. Come to that, he didn't want to sleep. He was still seething with anger. Not only at the way Allie had duped him but at the disappointment of the whole thing. To have been tricked like that, to have been fool enough to fall for it! He could hardly believe that he had been so gullible. But then, with a swift catch of breath, he remembered how sensationally beautiful she had looked splashing the water onto her body as she stood in the lake. The moonlight had silvered the wet silk that clung to her, the drops of flying water made into an arch of diamonds that shone brighter than the stars. She had looked like the goddess he'd called her, an ethereal being whose image would always be etched into his heart.

Drake groaned, realising just how easy it had been. She was a clever little witch who knew how to use the beauty of her body to seduce a man. And he made himself think of just how many men she must have been with to give her that kind of knowledge. She was a tramp. He was well rid of her. He should have followed his common sense which had warned him off her to start with. After all, there was always Emma to consider. But instead he had allowed his emotions—no, his concupiscence, nothing but that—to take over and had gone chasing after her. He'd thought, then, that it had been to take care of her and keep her out of trouble, but now he saw that it had been a challenge to his masculinity to find her, to make her admit that she wanted to go to bed with him.

Well, she had finally done so, he thought wryly, his mouth twisting in bitterness, but the surrender had been his, not hers; she had used and manipulated him all along. He turned onto his side and swore as the handbrake dug into him. He thought of where he could have been at this moment, beside Allie in the wooden bed, holding her glorious body in his arms, touching and exploring every part of her. She had been so willing, seemed so loving. She would have opened to him and he could have been inside her, loving her, lifting them both to the heights of passion. With a groan, Drake balled his fists and pressed them against his eyes, trying to shut out the pictures that tormented his mind.

At the same time, Allie was sitting hunched on the bed, still reeling from the shock of having her love thrown back in her face, but after a while, as she brooded over it, she began to feel angry herself.

Why couldn't Drake have listened, instead of going off like that? Not only hadn't he listened, but he had immediately jumped to the wrong conclusion, hadn't even paused for a second to think about it, let alone give her the benefit of the doubt. And that was because he hadn't had any doubts, she thought bitterly, completely forgetting that he had every reason to expect her to run away again at the first opportunity. Because the decision to give herself to him and the great surge of love she'd felt for him had been so overwhelming, so, conversely, was the chagrin and humiliation she felt now that it had all gone so horribly wrong. She had been prepared to humble herself for him, but now her pride had been terribly hurt, and there was no one to blame but Drake. She saw him now for what he was: chauvinistic, ungrateful, egotis-

tical; the list of derisive adjectives she could think of
to describe him seemed endless.

The picture of him, naked, his body hot and eager
for love, came unbidden into her mind and she flushed
in the darkness, determinedly trying to push the
thought away. It had just been sex, that was all. That
was all he'd ever wanted from her; Drake had as good
as admitted it when he'd first arrived. Picking up her
watch with its luminous dial, she saw that it was over
an hour since he'd gone out to his car, so there was
no way he was going to come back and apologise.
Grim-faced, Allie decided that she was glad he'd
turned against her. She hoped he'd leave early in the
morning so that she didn't ever have to see him again.

Lying on the hard seats that seemed to press into
him whichever way he tried to lie, Drake could still
think of nothing but Allie and what had happened
between them. His mind dwelt on her face when he
had caught her taking the keys from his pocket. She
had been surprised but there had been no consternation in her eyes. That puzzled him. Surely anyone
caught in the act of thieving would have jumped with
guilt, not turned with that wonderful smile of rueful
happiness? It hadn't been until she'd taken in the implication of his accusation that the smile had faded
into consternation.

And more than that. There had been appalled horror
in her eyes as she'd tried to talk to him. And what
had she said—that she'd realised that she cared for
him? Against his will a surge of something close to
hope entered his heart. But Drake had learned the hard
way not to trust hope; there had been too many

months and years of diminishing hope with Emma and he had come to find it the most treacherous of all emotions.

And anyway how could he possibly believe Allie, even if he wanted to? But that small flicker of hope refused to die.

Staring up into the darkness, Allie decided that she had been abysmally idiotic to fall for Drake and that she hated, loathed and despised him. And if she did see him tomorrow—and now she hoped she would—she would make it quite clear that he had been right, that she hadn't meant a word she'd said, and that she had seduced him just so she could steal the rotten keys and dump him. He hadn't liked that aspect of it, so she would rub it in as hard as she could. She felt angry and vindictive, ready to hurt as much as she had been hurt, and in that way try to reclaim some of her lost pride. And as the long night wore on so her anger grew.

And outside, looking out at the sky as the stars faded and the dawn began to break, Drake finally admitted to himself that he could have been completely wrong. He had to give Allie the benefit of the doubt and find out whether she had, for once, been telling him the truth. Because if she had... The errant ghost of hope refused to go, even began to grow. He so much wanted it to be true. He thought of going into the dacha straight away to sort it out, was eager to do so. But then he lay back; she would be asleep. It could keep for another couple of hours till morning. So he waited with growing anticipation, only needing her to say one word of welcome for him to take her back into his arms.

Unable to stand the discomfort any longer, Drake got quietly out of the car as soon as the sun began to rise on the horizon. He did some vigorous exercises to ease his cramped muscles, then walked up to the lake. A heron stood by its edge, poised and waiting to catch a fish. He watched it but the bird became aware of him and took off, skimming low across the water to the far side, its clumsy body graceful in flight. Going to the edge, Drake splashed cold water onto his face, trying to drive the woolliness from lack of sleep from his brain. One way or another, he felt that he was going to need all his wits about him this morning. He dried himself on his shirt, then put it on again, but without bothering to button it as he walked back to the dacha, wondering whether Allie was awake yet.

She was not only up but had washed, dressed and was collecting her stuff together ready to leave. Throwing back the curtains, she opened the windows to air the place. By the morning sunlight Allie found her nightdress, still on the floor where Drake had dropped it when he'd stripped it off her. Slowly, her feelings raw, she bent to pick it up and found that it was still damp. Her first reaction was to throw it away, but then something made her take it to the window and hang it over the sill to dry. It was as she was arranging it that the hairs on the back of her neck pricked. Quickly she looked up and saw Drake standing there, watching her with the strangest expression on his face.

For a long moment they just stared at each other, both silent, unwilling to be the first to speak. But then Allie remembered her resolve of the night, so, just as Drake opened his mouth to say something, she got there first and said tauntingly, 'I thought you were leaving.'

'I decided to wait until morning.'

'Well, don't let me keep you.'

Looking at her, studying her face, Drake saw that her mouth was set tight with tension and began to believe that her emotions *were* involved. 'I thought that maybe we could talk,' he suggested.

'Talk?' Her face hardened at his temerity. 'Just what makes you think I want anything more to do with you?'

Drake's hopes received a jarring blow, but weren't quite extinguished. Seeking a way through to her without coming right out and admitting that he thought he'd been wrong, he said carefully, 'Last night; maybe we could talk about what happened.'

'There's nothing to discuss,' she said shortly.

'But I think there is,' he persisted.

Allie had been about to retreat into the room, but now she stood still, wondering what all this meant. Then it came to her on a huge surge of rage. Her voice dripping with contempt, she said, 'What's the matter? Did you realise what you were missing and decide to stay for another try?'

It was so far from the truth and yet so near to it that Drake flinched.

Seeing it, Allie gave a derisive laugh. 'My God, you're so mixed up. You're crazy to have me and yet it all has to be on your terms. You wanted complete surrender but then thought you hadn't got it.' Losing her temper, she said vengefully, 'Well, for your information you were right. It was a set-up. Do you really think that I found you attractive enough to *want* to go to bed with you?' She laughed again. 'In your dreams!' And, stepping back into the room, she went to slam the window shut.

It was wrenched out of her hand, and the next moment Drake had vaulted through the opening and was standing menacingly in front of her. 'Say that again,' he demanded.

Too angry to be afraid, Allie put her hands on her hips and faced up to him. 'You heard me. What the hell makes you think I'd willingly have sex with a dull stick like you? You don't even turn me on. You never have. All I wanted was to get away from you.' Her mouth broadened into a sadistic smile. 'As a matter of fact I was going to take the keys and then tell you that I'd changed my mind, that I didn't want to go to bed with you after all.'

Hope shattered, Drake nevertheless said, 'Liar! You were more than ready for sex.'

Allie laughed on a triumphantly mocking note. 'Unfortunately there's no way of telling when a woman wants sex—unlike a man. And you were more than eager. God, you were so aroused, so frustrated, you were *panting* for it.'

Pushed beyond control, Drake snarled out, 'Yes, you're right. I was damn frustrated. And maybe I still am. Have you stopped to consider that?' He took a step towards her and Allie shrank back. Drake laughed. 'I can take you any time I want to. There's no one here to stop me. You certainly can't—even if you wanted to. And somehow I don't believe that you'd even try.'

He moved towards her again but when Allie backed away she came up against the table. She put her hands on it, staring at him, wondering if she had pushed him over the edge.

There was a hint of sadistic pleasure in the crease of Drake's mouth as he came close to her and put his hand under her chin. 'Why bother to fight me off? I'd be just another man, wouldn't I? Just another in a long list? There have probably been so many men that you've used that you can't even remember them any more. Or maybe you can; maybe you like to keep count. So tell me, Allie, how many men have you been to bed with to further your own ends?'

His assumption infuriated her so that she was no longer afraid. Pushing his hand away, she said curtly, 'Mind your own damn business.'

'Oh, I see,' he jeered. 'You've lost count. Well, that's hardly to be wondered at. But you played it badly, you know. If you'd waited until we'd been to bed together you could really have used me, had me eating out of your hand.'

'There are limits to how far I'd go,' she retorted contemptuously. 'Pretending an emotion I don't feel is one of them.'

'But going to bed with a man you don't want, using him, obviously isn't,' Drake said bitterly.

'That's right.' Pushing him aside, she moved a safe distance away and decided she'd better try finally to alienate him so that he'd leave in disgust. 'And I'll tell you why.' She paused, saw she had his attention, and said coldly, 'I work in a big city. If you're a single girl, and especially if you're a *successful* single girl in London, then you have two choices. You can try to find a relationship that means something, which usually means you end up bashing your head against a wall all the time, or you can behave the same way a man does, and go out and just have sex whenever you feel like it and with whoever takes your fancy.'

'You're talking about one-night stands.' Despite himself, there was shock in Drake's voice.

'That's right.'

His tone becoming glacial, he said, 'And I don't suppose I have to ask which road you've chosen to follow.'

'That's right,' Allie said again, her voice brittle. 'You not only don't have to, but you have no right to question me, either.'

'I beg your pardon,' Drake returned sarcastically. 'It's evident that I've made the biggest mistake in my life.'

'Right; you should have left last night.'

'Oh, not only in that; I meant in allowing myself to become attracted to a little tramp like you in the first place.'

It was too much for Allie. Swinging round, she glared at him. 'How dare you speak to me like that?'

'It seems to come very naturally.'

'You can talk! Of all the deceitful, underhand, two-timing liars...' Allie stopped to draw breath and to think up some other descriptive epithets she could throw at him.

Drake laughed in irony. 'You really know how to throw insults, don't you?'

'You don't do so badly yourself—and at least I have a reason.'

'What's that supposed to mean?'

But Allie was suddenly sickened by it all. She slammed her case shut, picked up her bag and headed for the door.

'Wait a minute! I asked you a question.'

'Oh… Just go to hell.'

She went to leave but Drake caught hold of her case. 'You're not going anywhere until I get an explanation.'

But she wouldn't answer, just said, 'Let go, damn you,' and they had a tug of war as they struggled through the doorway.

'I said let go,' Allie yelled.

'No, I damn well won't. I—'

They both suddenly broke off as a male voice behind them said, 'Good morning.'

Allie swung her head round, Drake straightened, dropping his end of the case, and they both stared in stunned surprise at the man standing just outside the house.

'Sergei!' It was Drake who recovered first. 'What—what on earth are you doing here?'

Sergei smiled in evident enjoyment of the situation, and gestured towards the sky. 'The weather is too hot for Moscow; I thought I would get away to the country.'

Drake suddenly tensed, his mind filled with the terrible suspicion that Allie might have come here for an assignation with the Russian. 'Are you saying that this is *your* dacha?'

'Mine?' The Russian laughed openly. 'No, no. It's not mine.'

His shoulders lowering, Drake said, 'Then—just how did you know where to find us?'

For answer, Sergei stepped to one side and gestured towards his car, which his large body had been obscuring. Ludmilla sat in the passenger seat, the baby on her lap, smiling at them as if she'd done them a big favour.

'When you both disappeared from Moscow so suddenly it occurred to me that you might be in trouble, so I thought I would look for you. I must admit that I had almost given up and was on the point of returning to Moscow, but then I happened to run into this lady who told me of the two foreigners who had rented one of the dachas.' He spread wide his hands, still grinning maddeningly. 'So, here I am.'

Allie couldn't find a thing to say, but decided there and then that she just wasn't cut out for anything at all adventurous and that when she got back to London she would never, ever leave its safety again.

But Drake merely glanced at the car and said, 'And presumably Ludmilla also told you that it had been rented by a married couple, by a husband and wife?'

'Yes, but the description she gave sounded so like you both that I decided to see for myself.'

Drake shook his head with a tut-tutting noise. 'Surely, Sergei, you are man of the world enough to know that you really shouldn't be surprised when two people run away to be together? And you should definitely never intrude into a love-nest? Should he, darling?' And then, to Allie's consternation, he went to her, put a possessive arm round her waist—and quite deliberately kissed her open mouth.

CHAPTER EIGHT

IT WAS Sergei's turn to look disconcerted. But only for a moment. Then he smiled again and said, 'You didn't sound like lovers a moment ago. In fact, you seemed to be very angry with one another.'

'Oh, that.' Drake gave an amused laugh and touched the suitcase with his foot. 'Allie thought the case was too heavy for me and she didn't want me to risk straining myself,' he said blandly. Then added, 'Isn't that right, darling?' and gave her an enquiring look.

Caught nicely in his trap, Allie could only nod speechlessly.

Going to the case, Sergei picked it up. 'It doesn't seem very heavy to me.'

'Doesn't it?' Drake sounded surprised, but then gave a rather smug smile. 'Strange—I don't seem to have much energy left this morning.'

The implication was very clear, and Allie found herself flushing as she met Sergei's eyes. It was probably the unexpected blush that startled him, made him wonder if they were telling the truth. He said, 'You're leaving?'

Allie said, 'Yes.'

But Drake said, 'No,' at the same moment. His fingers dug into her waist and he smoothed it over by saying, 'That is, we're leaving now to go into town to do some shopping, but if you mean are we leaving the dacha, then no, we're not. We plan to stay on possibly for another couple of days.'

'What made you choose this particular place?'

Drake shrugged. 'Pure chance. Allie came to have a closer look at the windmill, liked the area and phoned me to join her here.'

'So you didn't leave Moscow together?'

'No. I had some business to take care of first.' Drake decided he'd had enough of being interrogated and decided to attack. 'Why have you followed us, Sergei?'

The Russian smiled a little, then went across to the car and helped Ludmilla out, saw her on her way to her own house before saying, 'I was worried about you.' He gave an expansive gesture with his hands. 'First Allie leaves Moscow very suddenly, and then you. And I heard that you'd been making enquiries for a blonde woman travelling alone. As your friend, I thought I might be able to help you—in whatever it is that you came here to do,' he added with emphasis.

'That's very kind of you, but—' Drake gave an expressive shrug '—in the circumstances... Well, two's company and three's a crowd, and all that.'

Sergei frowned. 'I don't understand this expression.'

'Bluntly, it means that Allie and I want to be alone together, and I'm afraid you would be in the way.'

The two men looked at each other for a long moment, Sergei searching Drake's bland face for any sign of a lie, but Drake keeping his expression of man-to-man, slightly rueful amusement. But then Sergei's eyes went to Allie and saw the dark circles round her eyes, the strained expression in their depths.

'Allie doesn't seem to have much to say this morning,' he remarked, watching her closely.

Drake prodded her and she managed something approaching a panicky smile. 'Don't I? I suppose it's because—because I didn't get much sleep last night,' was the only thing she could think of to say. Immediately the words had left her mouth she realised their implication and blushed again.

Both men gazed at her face in fascination, and Sergei gave a small sigh, almost convinced at last. But then he said, 'If you are not leaving what are you doing with the suitcase?'

'Oh, it's just some clothes we're not using that we thought we'd keep in the car.'

'Then you must let me help you.' Sergei reached down and picked up the case. 'I should hate you to strain yourself,' he said to Drake with heavy-handed humour. Going to Allie's car, he jerked open the boot and lifted the case, then paused before putting it down on the ground again. 'Now I wonder why you need this?' And, reaching into the boot, he pulled out the spade that Allie had bought in the market.

Drake, not having known a thing about it, was temporarily lost for words. Allie's heart began to pound so loudly she thought they must hear it, and it was a moment before she managed to say in what was meant to be an offhand tone but sounded strangled even to her own ears, 'Oh, that. It came with the car.' She gave Sergei an innocent look. 'Don't all hire cars in Russia have them as standard—to dig yourself out of the snow?'

For a moment he looked taken aback. 'But it's summer.'

'Well, maybe they leave them in there all year. I don't know. Look, Sergei, it's lovely to see you but I'm afraid we don't have much here to offer you, so why don't you come into town with us and we can have a drink there?'

Again he seemed a little uncertain. 'That would be pleasant. Shall we go in my car?' he suggested.

'Fine. I'll just get my bag.'

She went inside and the next second Drake followed her and picked up his jacket. 'Remember we're supposed to be lovers,' he hissed at her as they went outside again.

Allie gave him a furious look, but managed to smile at Sergei when they went outside. 'I'll sit in the back,' she offered.

She expected Drake to sit in the front with the Russian, but instead he got in beside her and immediately put his arm round her, drawing her close. It wasn't far to the town, only a few miles, but they were some of the most traumatic Allie had ever known. She was worried about Sergei turning up, of course, but somehow that worry got lost beneath the feel of Drake so close to her. She knew she ought to want to push him away, but couldn't help liking his closeness, his warmth. But then, to her consternation, he put a hand behind her head and leaned forward to kiss her. Her fiery eyes met his in anger and she resisted him as much as she could, but then he whispered against her lips, 'Lovers. Remember?' and kissed her.

It was, she knew, all for Sergei's benefit, and didn't mean anything, but somehow that kiss got to her. Drake's lips were so insinuating, arousing a delicious sense of awareness, so that when he drew back Allie kept her eyes closed for a moment longer, and when they opened and gazed into his there was vulnerability in their blue depths. It changed to wariness but then he nuzzled her neck and her eyes closed again for a moment. When she opened them Allie found herself gazing into the driving mirror with Sergei's eyes staring back at her. She managed a small, uncomfortable smile, and the Russian quickly looked away.

Drake kissed her twice more in the short drive, and with each kiss Allie lost her inner resolve to resist him. OK, so it was all an act, but there was a difference between a token surrender for the sake of the game and the acceptance of a kiss as a kiss. Allie knew it—and so did Drake after he raised his head for the second time. But now Allie wouldn't look at him, lowering her face, although she allowed her head to remain on his shoulder. Those two kisses should have been enough to convince any observer that they were close, intimate, but Drake couldn't leave it there. He murmured her name and Allie slowly lifted her head but wouldn't meet his eyes. He touched the lobe of her ear with his lips, bit gently, and felt the tremor that ran through her. Her head turned with overborne reluctance, her eyes pools as dark as the lake, and then her lips parted as he bent to take them again.

Sitting in a café, drinking beer with Sergei, was both a reprieve and a torture. They talked about the weather, which had been fine for longer than anyone could remember but was reported to be about to break, and about almost anything but what was on their minds. Allie knew that she ought to be concentrating, making sure she didn't give anything away, but Drake evidently found it a necessary part of their pretence to hold her hand, to play with her fingers, and once even to raise her hand to his lips and look at her steadily, holding her eyes, while he kissed her palm.

After that, Allie felt almost giddy and unnerved, and was pleased when they finished their drinks and went to the store to buy groceries. Only they found that Sergei, too, had bought himself some basic foods.

Looking at them, Drake said, 'What's the idea, Sergei?'

'Oh, didn't I tell you? I like this area so much I've decided to stay here for a few days myself.'

His voice sharpening, Drake began to say, 'Look, I've already told you we want to be alone so—'

But Sergei raised a hand to stop him. 'Please, I understand. No, I have hired a dacha for myself.'

Still suspicious, Drake asked, 'Where?'

'It's on the road that leads to the place where you're staying. Just near the road. Everyone has to pass it, but it's very quiet, not like Moscow. When a car passes everyone looks out to see who it is.'

The implications were very clear; Sergei still didn't trust them and was going to watch them the whole time they were at the dacha.

When he dropped them off they watched him go a couple of hundred yards down the track and pull up beside another of the empty dachas. As he'd said, it was right by the road, and from its windows he would be able to watch them all day—and all night—long.

'How much do you bet he trained with the KGB?' Drake said feelingly. He turned to look at her, said softly, 'Allie?'

But her feelings were too mixed up for any kind of

confrontation and she said, 'Why don't we fix a picnic and have it by the lake?'

'OK.'

They quite openly carried a blanket and their food up the rise behind the dacha and sat under their favourite tree. 'Can he see us from here?' Allie asked nervously.

Glancing across at the other dacha, Drake said, 'I'm afraid so. And I think I caught the glint of the sun on binoculars.'

'The nerve!' Allie exclaimed. 'What the hell does he expect to see?'

'Us behaving like lovers, I hope.'

She gave him a sidelong look. 'You didn't have to tell him that.'

'I had to tell him something—and it seemed the obvious thing. What else would we be here for?'

'Touring around. Sightseeing.'

'Somehow I don't think Sergei would believe that.'

'I don't think he believes us now.'

'Better make it look convincing, then.' And Drake pulled her to him and kissed her, not letting her go for quite a while.

When they finally drew apart Allie slowly opened her eyes to find Drake looking down at her with the strangest expression in his grey eyes. 'For someone who says she hates me, that wasn't at all a bad effort,' he remarked with a smile.

Allie looked at him, was about to unburden her heart, but then changed her mind. 'It was purely to convince Sergei,' she said stiffly.

'Of course,' Drake returned smoothly. 'What else? How regularly do you think we ought to do it to make it look as if we really mean it? I should think every quarter of an hour on the quarter, wouldn't you?'

Despite herself Allie smiled. She turned from brushing away a fly to find that he was watching her again. 'You have the most wonderful smile.' Reaching out, he took hold of her hand. 'Do we have to go on hating each other, Allie?'

'You thought I'd deliberately set out to seduce you.'

'Was I wrong?' His voice was suddenly urgent.

'Don't you damn well know?'

'I know what I want to believe—but you haven't exactly been open with me.'

'Or you with me,' she flashed at him.

His mouth twisted into a rueful quirk. 'No, I suppose not. And I admit that I lied to you—about not caring about you. My feelings about you have been—overwhelming from the moment we met.'

Allie looked over the lake to where the sky was becoming dark, the air heavy and oppressive. 'You said that you wanted me from that moment.'

'Yes. Meeting you, seeing you every day, played hell with my libido—something I thought I'd got under complete control.'

It would have been a strange remark—if she hadn't known that he was engaged to someone else, had promised to marry another girl. Her face hardening a little, she said, 'So what are we talking about—sex?'

Letting go of her hand, Drake drew up his legs and rested his elbows on his knees. 'Maybe that's what it was to start with—an overpowering attraction. Until we kissed that first time. To be honest I wasn't sure how I felt about you until then. I think the physical need for you was so great that I couldn't see beyond it.' He paused. 'I desperately wanted to go to bed with you, have an affair with you, whichever way you want to put it. And I thought that once the urgency had gone out of it I'd be able to see more clearly, know if my feelings for you went deeper than that.'

'I see,' Allie said shortly. 'And if you'd decided they didn't, well, there was no harm done, was there? After all, we're only talking about *your* feelings here. Mine sure as hell don't seem to come into it.'

She went to get up, but Drake caught her arm. 'Please, Allie, let me finish.' He waited and she slowly sat down, eyes smouldering. Only then did he go on. 'I'm not the type who uses a woman, Allie. I tried to hold back, to not let you see how much I wanted you. I didn't want to coerce you in any way, which is probably why you accused me of being cold. But that night when we kissed I couldn't fight my feelings any longer. And it all seemed so right. You were so receptive, so loving. And I knew then that I wanted it to be far more than just an affair. I began to hope that you felt the same, that it might be for keeps.'

The sky suddenly grew very dark, but Allie didn't even notice. She turned to stare into his face, saw there only warmth and tenderness. But her voice grew bitter as she said, '"For keeps"?'

'Yes.'

'You mean a lasting relationship, do you? Living together, and all that kind of thing?'

He smiled a little and tried to take her hand. 'I mean that I love you. I mean getting married, Allie.'

Snatching her hand from him, she said with raw

hurt, 'Wouldn't that be a little difficult when you're already engaged to be married to someone else?'

Everything seemed to happen at once. Drake stared at her in appalled dismay. Allie got to her feet, prepared to run from him. And at the same moment there was a terrific crack of thunder and the heavens opened, sending down pelting rain that bounced off the hard earth, so thick and cold that it was like a curtain, at once transparent and yet difficult to see through, that was never still and had to be pushed aside as if it were something material. Within seconds they were soaked, their clothes clinging to their bodies, their hair to their heads. Jumping to his feet, Drake grabbed her hand and, abandoning the picnic things, began to run with her back to the dacha. Allie's foot slipped as the dust suddenly turned to mud and she went down on her knees. Turning, Drake lifted her easily into his arms, but she struggled, not wanting to be close again.

'Don't fight me!' He shouted the words in her ear above the storm. 'Don't fight me, my love.' And he bent his head to kiss her, oblivious of the blanketing rain.

When he straightened they had both forgotten everything but the hunger in his kiss, the desire it had aroused in them both. Allie stared into his tense face, then lifted a hand to run it down his cheek, to brush the raindrops from his chin. Only then did he go on and carry her into the house.

The sudden transition from oppressive heat to cold, from dryness to being soaking wet, made Allie start to shiver. She put her arms across herself and made no objections when Drake snatched up a large towel and began to rub her with it. He rubbed her vigorously at first, bringing warmth back into her, but gradually he slowed. Opening her eyes, she saw that he was gazing at her with open need, his face taut with the effort to control his hands, to stop them stroking her waist, her breasts. It occurred to her that she must look terrible, but suddenly she didn't care much, didn't care about anything but the knowledge that he'd said he loved her.

Softly, his voice little more than an urgent whisper, he said, 'You once promised to go to bed with me.'

'I know.'

'And do you keep your promises?'

Slowly she lifted her arms and put them round his neck, moved her body close against his, feeling him gasp and immediately harden. 'Yes,' she said on a sigh. 'Yes, I do.'

'Oh, God, Allie.' He suddenly clutched her to him and held her very close. 'I love you so much.'

She smiled up at him. 'And I you.'

He kissed her, kissed her passionately, but then straightened and said, 'I don't deserve that, not when I haven't even explained about Emma.'

'Who's Emma? Oh—your fiancée.' As she realised Allie put her fingers over his mouth. 'No, don't talk about that. Not yet. Now—now just love me.'

It was like one of those old-fashioned machines where you gripped the handles and it gave you an electric shock. Just the lightest touch of his fingertips on her skin sent wave after wave of delight coursing through her veins. Allie felt as if she had come alive for the first time in her life, and she clung to each exquisite moment of pleasure, never wanting it to end. But then his fingers would move on to find other, even more erotic places until her small cries of excitement became one long, panting moan of heightened awareness.

Drake undressed her with sure hands but taking off each garment slowly, kissing her as he went, his slowness both a delight and a torture. Kneeling on the bed, Allie lifted her arms above her head as he took off her T-shirt. He ran his hands down the length of each arm, warm, caressing, lingering to kiss her wrists, the inside of her elbows, her shoulders. Her head was back, her eyes closed, but she opened them languidly as he rained hot kisses on her throat. She sought his lips with her own and kissed him deeply, then took off his shirt and ran her hands over his smooth chest. Drake groaned, and reached behind her to unclip her bra and slip it off. The touch of his skin against hers was one of the most wonderful sensations Allie had ever known. Silk on satin. She felt him give a great quiver as she moved against him, her hands on his shoulders.

'Allie! Oh, my darling, I adore you.' He bent to kiss her breasts, cupping them in his hands as he lightly licked the pink aureoles around her nipples, but deliberately avoiding their heart, teasingly arousing her to growing hardness, until every tiny nerve-end was taut with longing.

It was unbearable. Allie put her hands in his hair and looked down at him with eyes that were dark with urgent desire. 'Please,' she whispered on a panting groan. 'Please.' And she moved so that he took her into his mouth, to thrill and delight her senses, to make her cry out with the exquisite torment of pleasure it gave her.

He delighted in her body, in running his hands along its length, in feasting his eyes on every curve, on every secret part of her. When they were naked on the bed, he kissed her lingeringly, caressed and stroked her until she was as aroused and eager as he, holding back his own urgent hunger because he wanted this to be as perfect for Allie as it was for him. Only when she cried out his name and arched towards him did he take her at last, riding the waves of passion and growing ecstasy until his thrusting body lifted them both to the heights of engulfing excitement.

For Allie it was the most wonderful emotional sensation of her life. Everything else, all other experiences in her past were as nothing, they faded from memory and were gone. There was only this glorious moment, the here and now in the arms of the man she loved. It was as if she had been cleansed and reborn. Her life began again from the minute he had taken her in his arms and loved her. She cried, and he understood and kissed away her tears, held her close and told her how precious she was to him, that his life was hers and he would love her till the day he died. Then he made love to her again with overwhelming joy.

It was already morning when Allie awoke and found that he wasn't beside her. She sat up in sudden terror, thinking it all a dream. 'Drake!'

'It's all right, I'm here.' He was immediately beside her, slipping into the bed and taking her in his arms.

She gave a sigh of relief. 'For a moment I thought it wasn't real.'

Drake grinned. 'Would you like me to prove that I'm real?'

She smiled, took his hand, and gently bit his bent knuckle. 'Mm. In a moment. First—tell me about the girl you called Emma. She is your fiancée, isn't she?'

Leaning back on the pillow, Drake sighed. 'She is and she isn't. She was, and I suppose always will be.'

'What? What are you talking about? I don't understand.' Pulling herself up, Allie leaned one elbow on the pillow and rested her head on her hand so that she could see him better.

But it also exposed her breast and the sight so absorbed him that Drake had to take the delicate bud in his mouth and feel it harden before Allie prodded him and he reluctantly let her go. Then he lay back on the pillow and said, 'Emma and I met when we were at university. We got engaged a couple of years later when we were quite young. We weren't in any hurry to get married; we were each working on our careers. And we didn't live together, although we both lived in London.'

His voice was quite matter-of-fact, but now he slowed as if he found the words difficult, and Allie guessed that what he was about to say wasn't pleasant for him. All kinds of things filled her mind, and she waited with curiosity all mixed up with dread for what he would say.

'One night Emma came over to my place and we made love,' he said heavily. 'I was going to get up and see her home, but she laughed at me, said she would be fine. Promised to get a taxi. It was a respectable neighbourhood. I thought she would be OK,' he said on a desperate kind of note. 'But there were no taxis around and she started walking. Some yobs saw her and tried to grab her bag. The police thought that she must have tried to hold onto it. So they hit her.'

His voice had become very bleak and Allie reached out to take his hand. He gripped hers so tightly that she had to hide a wince of pain. 'Was she badly hurt?'

'She was stunned and couldn't see. They pushed her and she stumbled into the road and was hit by a car. Was badly injured.' He paused for a moment then said sadly, 'She was in a coma for several months. When she eventually came out of it she wasn't my Emma any more. She was stuck in a wheelchair, unable to speak, all her vitality, her bright intelligence gone. And all for the sake of a few pounds,' he finished bitterly.

'Oh, Drake. I'm sorry. I'm so sorry. I had no idea. Bob just said that you had a fiancée, that you should have been home, visiting her.'

He stirred, came back from a deep, unpleasant picture of the past. 'She's in a nursing home, has the very best care. And I still go to see her regularly, along with her family and mine. But what hope there was has gradually disappeared. It's been hard to accept that she'll never get well. I know that I must let go, move on. Reason tells me that the girl I loved is dead, and she wouldn't have wanted me to just devote my life to a living corpse. But I clung onto hope.' He turned his head to look at her. 'Until I met you. You're so vital and alive. Sometimes, when we first met, that made me angry and jealous because you were whole and poor Emma is just an inanimate lump waiting to die. And I was angry because I wanted you so badly, too. Because I felt myself falling in love with you and I knew the time had come to let Emma go at last.'

Gently Allie stroked his hair back from his forehead. 'But you'll never let her go entirely,' she said in intuitive understanding. 'There will always be a place in your heart that's for her alone.'

'Would you mind that?'

She shook her head, said softly, 'I think I'd love you more for it.'

He smiled, kissed her nose, said, 'The strange thing is that you reminded me of her a little. Not in looks, but in your love of life. Being with you made me feel whole again, made me eager for each new day because I would be seeing you.'

'You didn't exactly give that impression,' she chided gently.

'No. You accused me of being austere, didn't you? But there were feelings of disloyalty that I had to come to terms with. I suppose they were feelings I should have faced up to ages ago, but I let them hang, so that when I fell so deeply for you I had to sort myself out in a very short time. I'm afraid that at times it wasn't easy.'

Able to imagine his distress, now that she knew what it was to love so deeply herself, Allie said, 'When did it happen?'

'Nearly seven years ago.'

'And how long was it before you stopped blaming yourself?'

He gave a small, bitter laugh. 'I don't think that will ever happen.'

'And is that why you were so protective of me back in Moscow?'

'I was terribly afraid something like it might happen to you. I don't think I could bear that—to have it happen twice in one lifetime.'

'Nothing will happen to me,' she assured him, leaning forward to kiss his forehead, to stroke his face gently.

He gave a sad shake of his head. 'You think you're immortal, that nothing will ever hurt you, and yet you blithely come over to Russia and risk everything on some crazy quest. Something you don't even trust me enough to tell me about.'

There was a trace of wryness in his tone and she quickly leaned over and kissed him. 'I do trust you. I'd trust you with my life. But it isn't my secret. Not really. But I think in these circumstances...' And she kissed him again.

'If you're going to tell me I think you'd better do so quite quickly,' Drake remarked, 'because if you go on kissing me my concentration level may be rather short.'

Allie chuckled and nestled into the crook of his arm. 'My great-grandmother was Russian and her family home was quite near here. She was a ballerina and often danced before the royal family. She was asked to give dancing lessons to the Archduchesses, and taught them for several years, but then the uprising came along. But my great-gran remained loyal to them and the last time she saw them, just before they were moved out of Moscow, the Empress gave her the four portrait miniatures of her daughters from the Clover Egg. It was to remember them by. It was all she had left to give.'

'So that's where the surprise went! Amazing. Was she able to keep it?'

'Sort of. A British man with a business in Moscow was in love with her. She managed to get back to her home and then he came and rescued her, smuggled her out of the country and married her. She lived to be very old and insisted that I was named Alexandra after the Empress. When I was a child she used to talk to me in Russian, tell me of her life here and of her escape. And just before she died she made me promise that I would come back and find the surprise.'

'Why didn't she take it with her?'

'They thought it would be too dangerous. If she was caught and the miniatures found she would have been killed for sure. So she buried it, in the garden of her family home.'

'So that was what the spade was for.'

'Yes.' She stroked her hand across his chest, watched his face as she said, 'Drake...'

He groaned. 'You'll get us both shot. What will you do with it if you find it?'

'My great-gran wanted me to keep it. She said it would be my inheritance from her. But...' She paused.

'But?' Drake prompted.

'I think I'd like to give it to the museum. It's part of Russia's past, not my family's. It belongs here.'

'I'm glad that's what you've decided. It's by far the best.'

'So when we dig it up we'll take it back to Moscow.'

'Of course you could just tell the authorities where it is and let them dig for it.'

She looked at him, her eyes on his face. 'Do you think I should?'

Drake grinned. 'No, I'm afraid I don't. I wouldn't be able to resist looking for it myself either.'

He was rewarded with one of her wonderful smiles. 'In that case,' Allie said magnanimously, 'I'll let you help.'

'Gee, thanks.' He pulled her to him. 'Now I think you wanted me to prove that I'm real.'

The rain lasted for two days, two long, wonderful days in which they didn't even emerge from the dacha, and the sun had been out again for several hours on the third day before they even noticed. Going to the window, Drake pushed it wide open and leaned on the sill to look out. Then said, 'Sergei! His car's gone.'

'Really?' Allie came to join him. Then pointed to the table under the overhang of the roof where a folded blanket and a pile of plates and glasses had appeared. 'Look, he must have collected up all our picnic stuff. But that means he must have been right outside while we were making love.' She looked at Drake unhappily. 'Do you think he was spying on us?'

'Possibly. But don't worry, he couldn't have made out individual words through the thickness of these walls. And whatever he did hear must have convinced him that we were only here as lovers, and he's left us alone.'

'Oh, I hope so.' She gave him a look of bright-eyed eagerness. 'When shall we try?'

'Better give it at least another day to make sure he doesn't come back.'

'Of course,' she said demurely. 'What other excuse would we have to stay here?' And with a gurgle of laughter she went into his arms.

They finally drove to the house that had once been her ancestor's home a couple of days later, in the early hours of the morning before dawn. The countryside was very rural, with just an occasional village. Allie had the diary her great-grandmother had written after her escape, which included a sketch-map of the area, on her lap. But the names of some of the places had been changed during the revolution and hadn't all returned to the old style. So it was almost an hour before they found the village that had been the nearest to the house.

With mounting excitement, Allie directed Drake along a lane between tall trees. 'According to Great-Gran's map we cross over a bridge and then the road follows the river down into quite a deep valley. On the modern map there's a lake nearby, but she doesn't mention that... Oh, look! We must be in the right place; there's the dome of a church off to the right. That must be where her family was buried. So the house must be just a short distance—'

They went round a bend in the road and they both gasped aloud. Ahead of them the road petered out on the shore of a vast lake, and off to the right the tower

of a church, surmounted by its onion dome, rose out
of the water, the rest of the building buried beneath
the grey waters that lapped at its stones.

For several minutes they stared in stunned silence,
then Drake said, 'This must be one of the reservoirs
Stalin had made to provide water for Moscow. I remember reading that he drowned over five hundred
villages.'

Slowly Allie got out of the car and walked down
to the edge of the huge lake. The dawn had broken,
the deep red of the sky reflected in the still, mist-laden
water. As the sun rose it cast shadows where the water
rippled on some objects close to the surface, and Allie
ruefully realised that they could be the chimneys of
the house she had come to look for. Now she would
never see the place where her ancestors had lived, or
be able to lay flowers on their graves, never be able
to walk down the village street that her great-
grandmother had described to her in such detail. And
she would never be able to gaze on the faces of the
portraits of the four young girls who had been her
pupils. The surprise would stay lost for ever. Allie
stood there for some time, feeling bitterly disappointed, but then, slowly and sadly, she began to think
that perhaps it was better this way; that world was
gone, had died in the cellar at Ekaterinburg.

Drake came to stand behind her and put his hands
on her shoulders. She gave him a misty smile as she
said, 'Maybe it's for the best. But I would have liked
to see the house where she lived, and especially the
garden. She used to tell me wonderful stories of her
life here as a child. I promised I'd come back, but
now it's too late, it's gone.'

'I'm sure she knows that you tried your best to keep your promise.'

'Oh, do you really think so?'

'Sure of it.' Putting his arms round her, he held her close for a while, then took her hand. 'Come on, my darling. It's time to go home.'

On the morning of her birthday, a few months later, Allie laughingly protested as her husband insisted that she stay in bed while he brought her breakfast up for her. It was a beautiful bedroom in a rather gorgeous house, because Drake had stunned her by turning out to be not just a glorified employee but one of the directors, with a large holding in the merchant bank.

He came in with the tray and on it she found a small parcel tied with ribbon. When she opened it Allie found inside the most intriguing bracelet on which were hung a dozen miniature but exquisitely made jewelled eggs. She stared and then her eyes flew to Drake. 'They can't be!'

Grinning, he nodded. 'Fabergé didn't only make eggs for the Tsar and his family.'

'Oh, Drake, it's beautiful. The most wonderful present.'

Throwing her arms round his neck, she kissed him in gratitude but the kiss was taken with passion. She drew back, laughing at him. 'Shall we move this tray?'

'I think we'd better.' He did so and drew her close again. 'You know something? I seem to remember you once called me a dull stick.'

'Did I?' She felt the hardness of his body and laughed richly. 'Well, that was certainly the misnomer of the century!'

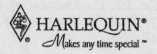

If you enjoyed what you just read,
then we've got an offer you can't resist!

Take 2 bestselling love stories FREE!

Plus get a FREE surprise gift!

Look for a new and exciting series from Harlequin!

HARLEQUIN
Duets ™

Two <u>new</u> full-length novels in one book, from some of your favorite authors!

Starting in May, each month we'll be bringing you two new books, each book containing two brand-new stories about the lighter side of love! Double the pleasure, double the romance, for less than the cost of two regular romance titles!

Look for these two new Harlequin Duets™ titles in May 1999:

Book 1:
WITH A STETSON AND A SMILE
by Vicki Lewis Thompson
THE BRIDESMAID'S BET
by Christie Ridgway

Book 2:
KIDNAPPED? by Jacqueline Diamond
I GOT YOU, BABE by Bonnie Tucker

2 GREAT STORIES BY 2 GREAT AUTHORS FOR 1 LOW PRICE!

Don't miss it! Available May 1999 at your favorite retail outlet.

HARLEQUIN®
Makes any time special. ™

Coming Next Month

HARLEQUIN PRESENTS®

THE BEST HAS JUST GOTTEN BETTER!

#2019 PACIFIC HEAT Anne Mather
Olivia was staying with famous film star Diane Haran to write her biography, despite the fact that Diane had stolen Olivia's husband. Now Olivia planned to steal Diane's lover, Joe Castellano, by seduction...for revenge!

#2020 THE MARRIAGE DECIDER Emma Darcy
Amy had finally succumbed to a night of combustible passion with her impossibly handsome boss, Jake Carter. Now things were back to business as usual; he was still a determined bachelor...and she was pregnant....

#2021 A VERY PRIVATE REVENGE Helen Brooks
Tamar wanted her revenge on Jed Cannon, the notorious playboy who'd hurt her cousin. She'd planned to seduce him, then callously jilt him—but her plan went terribly wrong: soon it was marriage she wanted, not vengeance!

#2022 THE UNEXPECTED FATHER Kathryn Ross
(Expecting!)
Mom-to-be Samantha Walker was looking forward to facing her new life alone—but then she met the ruggedly handsome Josh Hamilton. But would they ever be able to overcome their difficult pasts and become a real family?

#2023 ONE HUSBAND REQUIRED! Sharon Kendrick
(Wanted: One Wedding Dress)
Ross Sheridan didn't know that his secretary, Ursula O'Neill, was in love with him until his nine-year-old daughter, Katie, played matchmaker.... Then it was only a matter of time before Katie was Ross and Ursula's bridesmaid!

#2024 WEDDING FEVER Lee Wilkinson
Raine had fallen in love with Nick Marlowe, not knowing the brooding American was anything but available. Years later, she was just about to marry another man when Nick walked back into Raine's life. And this time, he *was* single!